I0535614

Backdoor to
the White House

THE 2016 ELECTION
AND THE CRAZY STORY
THAT MIGHT COME TRUE

CLARK VANDEVENTER

Copyright © 2016 by Clark Vandeventer

All rights reserved

The scanning, uploading, and distribution of this book via the Internet or via any means without the permission of the publisher is illegal and punishable by law. Please purchase only authorized print and electronic editions, and do not participate in or encourage piracy of copyrighted materials. Your support of the author's rights is appreciated. Of course, you are invited to share quotes from this book with attribution.

Cover design by Alex Tibio

Formatted for print and eBook
by manuscript2ebook.com

Edited by Lonnie Vandeventer

ISBN 978-0-692-76818-1

Contact the author and publisher at
BackdoorToTheWhiteHouse.com

Tweet to the author while you read.

Clark Vandeventer is on Twitter

@clarkvand.

You can find him on Facebook at facebook.com/ClarkOnPolitics.

#BackdoorToTheWhiteHouse

The characters in this book are real people but this is a fictional book. This is a hypothetical story of what *could happen.*
I am writing about potential future events.
Any quotes or actions taken by political figures are figments of my imagination.
I could see these people saying and doing these things, but you will have to ask them what they'll do if the 2016 Presidential Election ends without a winner.

CJV

For my father.

It's 12:01 AM on the East Coast, Wednesday, November 9th, 2016. The 45th President of the United States of America is yet to be determined. Forty-nine states and the District of Columbia have reported. No winner has been declared in the state of Ohio.

Hillary Clinton has 264 electoral votes. If she wins Ohio, Hillary Rodham Clinton will become the President of the United States. If Donald Trump wins Ohio, he will finish with 269 electoral votes; five more electoral votes than Clinton.

Perhaps you believe that if Trump wins Ohio, he will become the next president, but you would be wrong. You do not win the presidency by finishing in the lead. You win the presidency by winning a majority of electoral votes, and 269 is not a majority. It takes 270 electoral votes to become President of the United States.

Hours earlier, Gary Johnson, the Libertarian candidate for President, won his home state of New Mexico. By claiming 5 electoral votes, Gary Johnson may have just changed everything.

It all hinges on Ohio. If Hillary Clinton wins Ohio, she will finish with 282 electoral votes and will be elected President.

This book is a more than political fiction. This is not a far-fetched remote possibility. It is not a prediction of what will happen, but rather a story of what could happen. I have attempted to make this book as plausible as possible and to avoid political bombshells. Yet, every election is full of surprises. The political process is never predictable. I do not have a crystal ball, so I cannot predict with certainty what surprises the selection of the 45th President of the United States may hold, but I do know there will be surprises and so I've woven just a few into this story.

At 1:05 AM EST, all major media outlets report that they can now declare Trump the winner in Ohio.

What happens next?

CHAPTER 1

"FOX NEWS is now reporting Donald Trump to be the winner of the Ohio Primary."

"CNN can now declare that Donald Trump has won the state of Ohio."

"CBS can now confirm Donald Trump the winner in Ohio."

The words are still hanging in the air. The American people click through the channels looking for a commentator who can explain what happens next. This has never happened during our lifetime. In 2000 George W. Bush lost the popular vote, but won the Electoral College. The hanging chads in Florida during that election were confusing enough. Some may remember newspaper headlines declaring "Dewey Defeats Truman," but once you could get over the fact that the press was overanxious to declare a winner, that election was easy to figure out. Now, here we are in the early morning hours of November 9th. The 2016 Election is over. All the votes have been casts and counted and there is no winner – no candidate has successfully reached the 270 electoral vote milestone.

Shortly after Gary Johnson was declared the winner in New Mexico, the networks tried to find talking heads who could explain what would happen if no candidate hit 270. There was confusion and even ambiguity. Nobody had thought about this in a long time, it seemed.

Two times in our county's history the Electoral College had failed to produce a winner - 1800 and 1824.

In 1800, Thomas Jefferson and Aaron Burr ended in a tie. The writers of the Constitution had not anticipated the formulation of political parties and to expedite the process of selecting a president, voters in the Electoral College were instructed to vote for two candidates for president. The candidate with the most votes would become president. The candidate with the second most votes would become vice-president.

However, in 1800 Thomas Jefferson and Aaron Burr ran as a ticket under the banner of the Democratic-Republican Party. The Democratic-Republicans devised a plan where each person would cast their votes for Jefferson and Burr, with one person abstaining on his second vote. The idea was that this would allow Jefferson to finish with one more vote than Burr, and therefore Jefferson would become president and Burr vice-president. The plan was botched, though, and Jefferson and Burr ended in a tie.

The election then went to the House of Representatives as defined in the U. S. Constitution. On the 36th ballot in the House, Jefferson was elected the 3rd President of the United States.

After the Election of 1800, the 12th Amendment to the Constitution was passed. The 12th Amendment outlines the procedure to follow if the Electoral College fails to produce a president. The 12th Amendment is the answer to the question of what happens now that it's November 9th and neither Donald Trump nor Hillary Clinton have won the election.

The 12th Amendment has only come into play one time in American history. In 1824, Andrew Jackson won the popular vote and also finished with the most electoral votes, however he failed to receive the necessary number of electoral votes to win the election. The election then went to the House of Representatives where the House selected the man who had finished second in the Electoral College, John Quincy Adams, to become president of the United States.

That didn't sit well with Andrew Jackson and his supporters, as you may have guessed.

Now it's a little past 1:00 AM on November 9th and we are waiting on both Clinton and Trump to address supporters. What will they say?

The talking heads are trying to explain the 12th Amendment. The election of the 45th President of the United States now goes to the newly elected House of Representatives. The 435 men and women who just won election and who will be seated in the House of Representatives on January 3rd are the 435 men and women who will select the next president.

But it's not that simple. Each state votes by State Delegation. So the fifty-three newly elected representatives from the State of California will vote as a block. The fifty-three representatives from the State of California count as one vote. South Dakota only has one congressional representative. The lone member of the House of Representatives from South Dakota is equal to fifty-three from California. South Dakota gets one vote. It takes 26 votes in the House to become president.

The House can select from and only from any of the top three finishers in the Electoral College, Donald Trump (269 electoral votes), Hillary Clinton (264 electoral votes), and Gary Johnson (five electoral votes).

The panel on FOX NEWS is dissecting the congressional delegations state-by-state with a camera fixed on both Trump's and Hillary's campaign headquarters. It's nearly 1:30 AM, but we are expecting both candidates on stage at any moment.

Former New Mexico Governor Gary Johnson has already spoken. Just after his win in New Mexico, he appeared before an exuberant crowd in Santa Fe and declared the two-party system in America to be dead. "This changes everything," he said to tremendous applause. At that moment, Gary Johnson knew he would end the night with only five electoral votes, but he took the stage like a conquering hero. In winning New Mexico Johnson has already done something no other 3rd party candidate has done since 1968 when former Governor George C. Wallace won forty-six electoral votes.

"We will await the voter's decisions in the remaining states yet to report and if there is no winner tonight, we will fight hard in the coming weeks to make the case that I am most fit and most prepared to be the next President of the United States."

Those words brought about a thunderous reaction in Santa Fe, but most people at home watching Gary Johnson on TV had no idea what he was talking about. He won New Mexico. It's five electoral votes. Who cares?

But as one state after another reported it became clearer what Gary Johnson was talking about. The person with the most electoral votes does not win. It takes a majority of electoral votes -- 270 to win. With Gary Johnson winning those five measly electoral votes in New Mexico, nobody was going to hit 270.

How had the national media missed this story? For weeks Gary Johnson had been appealing to New Mexico's voters on the basis of their ability to be spoilers. "Nobody takes us serious," Johnson would say at campaign rallies in New Mexico, where he spent 16 of the last 21 days before the election. New Mexico ranks 36th out of the 50 states in population. Johnson appealed to their ability to be #1 in power.

"ABC News has learned that Hillary Clinton will not be addressing supporters tonight."

"NBC News is hearing reports that Donald Trump will not be speaking tonight."

"We just received a statement from Hillary Clinton's press secretary. Hillary Clinton will not be making an appearance tonight."

"Donald Trump will not be addressing supporters tonight."

It's nearly two o'clock in the morning now. There's so much confusion that advisors to both Trump and Hillary have convinced them to not make any remarks. It seems this election will go to the House of Representatives. There's too much at risk now. Don't want to possibly say something at this late hour that could offend a House member -- a solitary vote necessary to secure the presidency. Best to go to bed and begin working on the

House in the morning.

But when Donald Trump learns that Hillary will not speak, he sees an opportunity to have all eyes on him.

While it is approaching 2 AM on the East Coast, it is only 11 PM on the West Coast. People are still awake. People are glued to their televisions trying to figure out what's going to happen next. Those who've already gone to bed, they can wake up in the morning and the first thing they'll see is Donald Trump making his case. The news channels will play clips of Donald Trump while reading a statement from Hillary's press secretary.

"Wait, we have just received word that Donald Trump will take the stage in New York City shortly."

"Donald Trump is now taking the stage in New York City."

"What a tremendous night and thank you for being here. I can't believe how many of you have stayed so late. Wow! What a night. It's two o'clock in the morning, but that's okay. I have energy. I can stay up until two o'clock in the morning unlike Crooked Hillary who couldn't take a phone call at three in the morning. Look, we didn't get to 270 electoral votes tonight, but that's okay. We'll get there. I am going to be the next president. We have tremendous friends in the House and they will do the right thing. I know they will do the right thing because we are going to make America great again. That I'll tell you. We are going to make America great again. The next step is the House and we will win there because we have tremendous friends in the House who want to make America great and they know that Hillary is not going to do that. Look, it's going to take some time to get where we want to be, but we have come a long way. What a tremendous campaign. So many wonderful people. We won states that nobody thought we could win. We won them. We had huge turnout in states that people said I could never win and we won them. We won them. And I am going to win the presidency that I can tell you. I will be the next President of the United States and I am excited to go to work at making America great again. Thank you."

CHAPTER 2

"Speaker of the House Paul Ryan has a press conference scheduled for this morning at 11:00 AM in Janesville, Wisconsin, where he easily won re-election last night in Wisconsin's 1st District. It seems that Ryan will retain his job as Speaker of the House. Republicans maintained control of Congress last night, but he will operate with a slimmer majority due to the loss of some Republican held seats. We're standing by here at FOX NEWS and will go to Janesville as soon as Speaker Ryan takes the podium."

The Republicans were not annihilated in the House on election night. In all, the GOP lost a net of thirteen House seats. In the House of Representatives, the election of 2016 did not reveal a colossal shift in American politics. For the most part, Democrats held Democratic seats and Republicans held Republican seats. However, a handful of Republicans could not survive one simple question, "Are you voting for your party's nominee for President?" It didn't even matter how they answered the question. The fact that the question was being asked was evidence enough that they were doomed.

Republican Paul Ryan would lead a smaller, though still strong, majority in Congress, with Republicans outnumbering Democrats 234 to 201. Donald Trump has reason to be confident, but more reason than you may yet understand.

"We're going to Janesville, Wisconsin right now where Speaker Paul Ryan is ready to speak."

"Good morning. Last night the American people witnessed a truly historic election, and in the coming weeks, the American people will again play witnesses to history. After the election of 1800, our nation's leaders recognized a flaw in the process for electing the president of the United States. Today, Thomas Jefferson is a revered figure in American history. I have on more than one occasion found myself standing in the rotunda of the Jefferson Memorial in Washington seeking inspiration from this architect of the American ideal. It is little remembered that Thomas Jefferson actually became president after he failed to win the Electoral College outright and that it took 36 ballots in the House of Representatives before he was elected president."

"After the election of 1800, the 12th Amendment of the Constitution was ratified, which amended the process of how the president is elected and what happens should the Electoral College fail to produce an outright winner, as it did last night. Since the 12th Amendment to the Constitution was ratified, it has only been needed one time, and that was almost 200 years ago in the election of 1824."

"When the Electoral College failed to produce a winner in the election of 1824, the selection of the next president went to the House of Representatives, and the House elected John Quincy Adams as our 6th president."

"At the beginning of my remarks I said that last night the American people witnessed history. In the coming weeks, the American people will again play witness to history. It's been 192 years since this has happened. Your parents never experienced this. Your grandparents never experienced this. Your great-grandparents never experienced this. Your children and your grandchildren and your great-grandchildren will likely never experience this."

"There is a lot of confusion this morning. A lot of people are wondering what happens next. Some people feel lost. We had an election last night that produced no winner, and while we all expected to wake up this morning and know who will be the next President of the United States, that did not happen."

"But there is no reason to feel lost or confused because the 12th Amendment to the Constitution outlines our exact duties from this moment forward.

On December 19th the Electoral College will meet in all 50 states, along with the District of Columbia, to cast their official ballots for President of the United States. The newly elected Congress -- the 115th Congress -- will meet on January 6th in a Joint Session of the House and Senate to officially count the votes and ratify the result.

Barring a change in the electoral vote between now and when the Electoral College votes on December 19th, after January 6th the House of Representatives will choose from the top three candidates in the presidential election who will be our next president. The Constitution limits us to these three candidates, and only these three candidates."

"I would like to congratulate Donald Trump, Hillary Clinton, and Gary Johnson for the campaigns they have run. These are the three candidates the members of the House of Representatives will be able to consider to be our next president."

"As prescribed in the 12th Amendment, the House will vote by State Delegation with each state counting as one vote. A candidate must receive a majority of votes, meaning that to be elected president a candidate must receive at least twenty-six votes."

"The next Congress will begin session on January 3rd, and we obviously have a very important item of business on our agenda. This election is a process I promise you we will take very seriously with a clear conscious and a quiet heart before God. As Speaker of the House, I will view it my utmost responsibility to ensure that the process of electing the next president is done so in strict accordance to the Constitution."

"We will leave it to our colleagues in the Senate to elect the vice-president. The 12th Amendment stipulates that the vice-president be selected from among the top two candidates for vice-president. As is the case in the House, the new Senate will begin session on January 3rd and it will be this newly elected Senate that will select the vice-president."

"I would ask all Americans to pray for our country, our candidates, and our Congress as move forward in this process together. Thank you."

"Let's go to Santa Fe."

"Shouldn't we call him first?"

"Call Bill and ask him to make sure they're ready for us."

It was unprecedented for a party's nominee in one presidential election to refuse to support the nominee that followed him just four years later. That's exactly what happened with this election. Mitt Romney, the 2012 Republican nominee for president made no secret of his feelings for Donald Trump.

"Think of Donald Trump's personal qualities. The bullying, the greed, the showing off, the misogyny, the absurd third grade theatrics," Romney said of Trump in a last ditch effort to sway his party from nominating Trump for the presidency. He called Trump a con man, a fraud. He said a promise from Donald Trump was about as good as a degree from Trump University and accused him of playing the American public for suckers.

Those are some pretty harsh words from a pretty mild mannered guy.

Trump responded by calling Romney a lightweight and the crowds loved him for it.

Now Mitt Romney wants to go to Santa Fe to talk to Gary Johnson.

There were rumors leading up to the election that Romney would endorse Johnson, but the rumors never materialized. Johnson's vice-presidential running mate, Bill Weld, served as Governor of Massachusetts six years before Romney and campaigned for Romney when he ran for president. "If Bill Weld were at the top of the ticket, it would be very easy for me to vote for Bill Weld for president," Romney said on CNN in June. Romney spoke favorably of Johnson on numerous occasions, but came short of issuing a formal endorsement.

Romney's not going to call Gary Johnson first. He wants to get to Santa Fe now. "Call Bill and ask him to make sure they're ready for us," is as much as he's willing to stall. Romney's staff puts in a call to Governor Bill Weld. "Tell Gary to meet us at the airport."

Some might say Mitt Romney is a loser. He couldn't beat John McCain to win the Republican nomination in 2008 and he wasn't even close to beating Barack Obama in 2012. Still, about 60 million people voted for him. That's a lot more people than have voted for Gary Johnson.

It's Wednesday morning after the election and Johnson, like Clinton, has so far been silent. Cable news shows are showing Trump's election night speech over and over again. Hillary Clinton is scheduled to speak in the afternoon, but the pundits are starting to paint a gloomy picture of her path to the presidency.

Hillary Clinton has 264 electoral votes, just five fewer than Donald Trump, but still six votes short of winning the presidency. She is leading in the popular vote, however, and received roughly six million more votes than Donald Trump. She did not win a majority of the popular vote, as Hillary finished with only 41 percent of the popular vote. Donald Trump finished with 38 percent and Gary Johnson pulled in 20 percent. At 20 percent Johnson bests all third party candidates since the Civil War except that of former President Theodore Roosevelt when he ran under the Progressive "Bull Moose" banner in 1912.

Still, Hillary wouldn't be the first Clinton to win the presidency with less than a majority of the popular vote. Her own husband Bill Clinton was elected in 1992 with only 43 percent of the popular vote.

While 41 percent is less than a mandate, her bigger problem lies in the House of Representatives. The 115th Congress that will select the 45th president has 33 more Republicans than Democrats. That's bad news for Clinton, but what's even worse is that Republicans control the state delegations in multiple states that she won.

Virginia, for example, is a state that Clinton won, but of the nine congressional representatives from Virginia five are Republicans. Clinton won Pennsylvania, but Pennsylvania has eleven Republicans and seven Democrats in its House delegation. These are two states that she won that will likely vote against her in the House.

Pundits point out that Republicans outnumber Democrats in 31 states. Democrats hold the advantage in only 17 states. In two states Republicans and Democrats are divided equally. If it takes 26 votes in the House to be elected president, what states does she hope to win? How does she get to 26? What Republican members of Congress does she hope to sway? Republican members of Congress know that if they vote for Hillary Clinton for president, they will never win re-election; they'll be opposed, and will lose, in a primary. How does Hillary keep Donald Trump from winning on a first ballot in the House of Representatives, which is exactly what will happen if the state delegations in the House vote among party lines?

Meanwhile, across the country Romney's plane touches down in Santa Fe. News cameras from all over the world are fixed on Mitt Romney and Gary Johnson as they shake hands and Romney turns to address the press.

"My friend Bill Weld has told me many good things about Governor Johnson. I look forward to sitting down with him and getting to know him better."

"Last night we won 20 percent of the popular vote," Johnson says. "I'm grateful to the many Americans who supported our campaign and our effort to destroy the two-party system. I want to thank the voters of New Mexico for changing the electoral map in a very big way. We are on the verge of making history, and I want to thank Governor Romney for coming down here to Santa Fe to talk with me. We have some big things to discuss."

Reporters shout questions, but both Romney and Johnson shrug them off as if it's just the two of them alone for a walk in the park. They walk to a black Suburban, get in the back, and drive off into the desert.

CHAPTER 4

Footage of Donald Trump's election night speech dominated the early morning news. That was followed up by discussions of Clinton's difficult path to the presidency in a Republican controlled House. Now all the cameras are on Gary Johnson and Mitt Romney in New Mexico.

Back in New York, Hillary Clinton is livid. "We are fucking losing."

"How the hell did we not see this coming? He's a showman. He loves the stage. Of course he was going to speak after we announced that I wouldn't! How in God's name did we issue that statement? We basically invited him to upstage us!"

"We're sitting here with our thumbs up our asses while those fucking assholes dance circles around us."

Her staff has gotten the message and are ready to spring into action.

Joel Benenson and Amanda Renteria, two top Clinton strategists and confidants, start talking.

Renteria has her mind made up. "We're going to Monticello. You need to speak and we need a historic backdrop. Everyone's talking about this being a historic election now. You're the historic candidate."

"And we need Virginia," Benenson adds. "We can get Virginia."

Hillary won Virginia on election night, but the House Congressional Delegation is controlled by Republicans. It's a very close split, though. Five Republicans to four Democrats after the Democrats picked up a seat on election night. Terry McAuliffe, a longtime Clinton insider and former Democratic National Committee Chairman, is the governor. It's an increasingly Blue State and Republicans have manipulated the political system and drawn district lines to hold onto power.

Hillary is ready. "Set it up. Trump had the morning and Johnson is having his moment now, but we will dominate the evening news."

"We can do it at 3 o'clock. It's great timing." And Renteria is out the door to get everyone working on Monticello.

Now Benenson and Hillary really get down to business.

"We need Gary Johnson, Hillary," Benenson says solemnly. "It's a damn good thing he actually won New Mexico. We need him in this."

"Look, Hillary," Benenson continues, "There are some state delegations we are never going to win. Virginia, Pennsylvania, Michigan, we can make a run at those. But, before we can win, we have to make sure Trump does not win. We've got to work to get a few of these states that are never going to vote for you and convince them to go for Johnson."

"We need to get Pelosi in here. We've got to make sure there is not an inch of wavering among Democrats in the House. Let the Republicans and the Johnson people fight it out." Benenson is now speaking more confidently, a cadence is forming in his speech. "If any Democrat is less than enthusiastic in their support, they will never hold office again. We will bury them. The problem with the Republicans, they know that if they support you they'll never have a chance of winning re-election. But, some of these people hate Trump more than they hate you. We need to offer them support. Get them to switch parties. There are a few Republicans in Democrat leaning districts that would have a better chance getting re-elected if they switched parties and supported you."

It's quiet. Hillary is pacing around the room. Without saying it directly, Benenson is confirming what the pundits have been saying on TV. She has a difficult path to the presidency in the House. But she's not downtrodden. Her confidence is growing. She takes in a deep breath and her resolve grows. Benenson's excitement is building as he sees Hillary's confidence take control.

"We need to pick off someone," she says. "We need a Republican we can put on TV who's defected. Trump has set himself up for this, running away from his own party, and his own party running away from him. He couldn't even get the Bush's to support him and they have hated Bill and me since 1992."

"We'll find one," Benenson says without hesitation. "We may have to offer something."

Clinton quietly comes back, "Do what you need to do."

"It's okay for Johnson to pick up a few votes as long as Trump is losing them. We can't lose any. But when Trump starts losing states on both ends, he'll look weak."

Renteria is back. "They're ready for us in Monticello. Secret Service is already there and they are getting things in place to move us. Press has been notified. We've got the speechwriters working."

◆

Behind closed doors on Wednesday morning, Hillary Clinton looked like she was about to come unglued. She was out of control, erratic. Now, she is calm. Suddenly, she seems presidential. There's a quiet resolve about her. It's as if she is facing the first crisis of her presidency -- a crisis of whether she will become president at all -- and all of the wisdom of her vast life experience is now kicking in.

She's at Monticello now. Monticello, the home of Thomas Jefferson. Thomas Jefferson, the author of the Declaration of Independence. Thomas Jefferson, whose writings asserted long before the idea was palpable, that all men *and women* are created equal. Thomas Jefferson, the father of the Democratic Party. It's where the Jefferson comes from in her husband's name, William Jefferson Clinton.

Bill is by her side now. They are alone, or as alone as the Clinton's have been for almost twenty-five years. Hillary and Bill stand quietly with a Secret Service detail around them. Terry McAuliffe is in front of the cameras and he's warming up the crowd. McAuliffe is setting the stage, talking about why Clinton has chosen Monticello as the backdrop for her first appearance after the election.

McAuliffe lets the anticipation build. The truth is, he loves the attention. He's a little resentful of the fact that he's spent most of his life being the Clinton's bagman, but he's also proud of the fact. Being Governor of Virginia vindicated him in his own mind. He was more than a bagman. Today, he's a bagman, though, and it feels like old times.

"We really should get out there before Terry says something we regret," Bill says with a laugh. Hillary doesn't answer, she just starts walking. Bill falls in step with her, and now she stands before a throng of press, cameras rolling and flashes clicking.

Clinton's speech is slow and steady. She speaks with resolve. Her words, measured. She borrows from Jefferson.

Hillary Clinton's entire campaign was anti-climactic. It seemed that her moment, if she was to have one, was eight years ago. 2008 was when she appeared to have hit her high-water mark. The moment that was supposed to be her's turned out to be Barack Obama's. Her 2016 campaign lacked energy. She was the first woman to be nominated for president by a major political party, but the moment barely seemed like a celebration. The energy in the Democratic Party was not with Hillary; it was with Bernie. Clinton was a logical choice. Like trading your blue Jeep for a nice Chrysler LeBaron. Voting for Hillary Clinton was what grown-ups do.

Now Hillary looks like a president. She looks like the person you would want to have their hand on the wheel.

She took questions. Clinton never takes questions. She lingered with the press. She looked relaxed. Bill told a few jokes and got in some digs on Trump. He reminded people how great life was when he was president. He even made a disparaging remark about Newt Gingrich for old time's sake.

For so long Hillary Clinton has wanted to be president. She has wanted it more than the air she breathes. She knows the situation in the House. She knows the odds are against her. In her mind, she's already lost, and it's made her incredibly relaxed. If she can pull this off, it would be a joyous surprise.

The best Hillary Clinton has ever looked on the campaign trail was in 2008, after it started to become clear that she would lose to Barack Obama. That Hillary seemed vulnerable, approachable, and even relatable.

On Wednesday, November 9th, that's the Hillary Clinton we see again.

CHAPTER 5

The black Suburban carrying Mitt Romney and Gary Johnson leaves the Santa Fe Municipal Airport and turns north onto Interstate 25. Now well out of the city, the car turns onto Highway 50 and eventually pulls up to the exclusive Brush Ranch River Lodge. Johnson's running mate, Governor Bill Weld emerges from a cabin just as the Suburban comes to a stop.

Weld and Johnson share a glance and Weld turns to his old friend Mitt Romney. The two men shake hands, laugh, and then embrace. Weld then turns to lead the group of three former governors into a cabin for a fireside chat.

A contingent of reporters followed the governors from the airport to Brush Ranch. Now, the group is growing.

"Thank you for flying down, Mitt. You sure have brought a lot of attention with you," Johnson says as they sit down by the fire.

"You brought the attention with what you did last night," Romney responds. "Listen," Romney continues,

"Yesterday, when I went to the ballot box and I had to cast my vote for President of the United States, I voted for you. You were the only candidate on the ballot I could vote for with a clear conscious. It was a personal decision. I never expected that you'd hit 20 percent or that you'd win a state, or that we'd be sitting here today with it looking like this election is going to the House."

There's an awkward silence and Johnson finally jumps in. "Well, thanks Mitt. It means a lot to me to have gotten your vote."

Romney puts up his hand softly to say he's not quite finished. "I woke up this morning feeling sick. I wondered what could have happened if I'd done more. Sure, there are people who speculated I was voting for you, but what if I'd come out with my full support? Could that have encouraged a couple of Republican members of Congress to do the same? Could you have picked up an extra two percent of the popular vote? An extra five percent? Could you have won Utah? Nevada? Alaska?"

It's clear that Romney means every word he's saying with every fiber in his being. Johnson is moved. "You don't need to worry about any of that, Mitt. We're here now."

Weld jumps in. "What do you have in mind, Mitt?"

"I want to do whatever I can to help. I called Paul Ryan on the way down here. He's the Republican leader and has to support Trump, but he promised me a fair process in the House. And when we walk out of this meeting today and the cameras meet us, I'm going to say unequivocally that you should be the next president. There was no winner last night, our country is divided and the major parties have nominated two unpopular and highly divisive figures. I'm going to call on both parties in the House to set aside politics and do what's right for the country."

Johnson is shocked. "That would mean a lot, Mitt, and would be a signal that last night really did change everything. You ready to do this?"

"Well, we can't just walk out there now," Weld says with a laugh. "We've got to string them along a little bit."

There's actually a lot more to talk about. Romney writes out a list of House members he campaigned with in his two runs for the White House and who he may be able to influence. They talk about the next few days, where they're going, who they're meeting with.

"You chose a good running mate," Romney adds. "I doubt I'd be here without Bill."

The cabin doors open and out walk the three governors. Mitt Romney is first to speak, and he speaks with emotion. He wishes he'd done more to support Johnson before the election and confesses that he hedged in his own political self-interest. He acknowledges that he and Johnson don't agree on everything, but that he believes Gary Johnson is most ready and most prepared to be the next President of the United States.

He addresses the fact that Johnson finished in last place in the popular vote, but questions how many Americans would vote differently if they knew that this really was a three-person race. He says the major political parties have lied to us and duped us into believing that a vote for a third party candidate is a waste of a vote.

Romney looks like a statesmen. He seems more like the man you want telling you who should be president than the man who you want to be president. He feels trustworthy. A man with nothing personal to gain. A man speaking from his heart out of love for his country.

Johnson is now at the mic. Although he spoke after winning New Mexico, this is the first time he's addressed reporters, and the nation, since it became clear just how much his win in New Mexico had changed everything. He pledges to fight on. He declares that his victory in New Mexico was the first of many victories. "People now know that they're not stuck with Clinton or Trump. That knowledge is power, and that power is what is going to fuel our campaign to victory."

Bill Weld speaks and acknowledges that he knows he will not be vice-president. The Senate will choose from among the top two candidates for vice-president, Republican Mike Pence and Democrat Tim Kaine. Still, he considers himself to be Johnson's running mate. He's there for him and ready to do anything he can to get Gary Johnson to the White House.

It's time to wrap things up. "I have a flight to catch," Johnson says. Reporters ask where he's going.

"South Dakota."

CHAPTER 6

"Who the hell is this guy? He's a joke."

Donald Trump is watching Gary Johnson on television and is completely baffled. The mood in the Trump campaign is almost euphoric. Although he fell one vote shy of winning the Electoral College, Republicans control a strong majority of state congressional delegations. If the state delegations vote along party lines, Trump has 31 votes, five more than he needs to secure the presidency. They fully expect to get 31 votes. No Republican will ever vote for Hillary Clinton, and Johnson is delusional to think he is somehow going to get to 26 votes in the House.

The Trump campaign is so confident that they have entered transition mode. He's in Washington now, and throughout the next week has meetings scheduled with campaign surrogates who are ready to cash in their presidential appointments. For good measure, he's scheduled a breakfast for tomorrow morning with the Republican leadership in the House. Republican National Committee Chairman Reince Priebus is declaring the

2016 election a complete victory for Republicans. "We've won the presidency and maintained our majorities in the Senate and the House of Representatives," Priebus said to reporters who pushed him on GOP losses in Congress. The American people have entrusted both Houses of Congress to the Republican Party and soon we will confirm that Donald Trump is our next President." Privately, Priebus feels great relief. He managed to lead his party through an election with a polarizing figure at the top of his ticket. Fifty-one seats in the Senate is barely a majority, but he'll take it.

"Lightweight. He's a lightweight," Trump says mockingly at the TV, in reference to Mitt Romney. What a sad, sad guy. A complete failure as a candidate. And now he thinks he's going to get this joker in the White House." Trump is loose and he is confident, and sees no contradiction in calling Romney a failed candidate even though Romney received more than 13 million more votes for president in 2012 than Trump got yesterday.

Trump already gave his victory speech last night. He has the votes in the House. In his mind, he's now the presumptive President of the United States, and it's time for everyone else to get on board with this idea. They finally accepted the fact he was the presumptive nominee because he had the votes and now he's the presumptive President because he's got the votes.

Hillary Clinton is now viewed with what could almost be described as sympathy. The TV is now showing highlights from Hillary's speech at Monticello. "What's she doing? She should be in jail! She's a loser." Hillary received 4 million more votes than Donald Trump last night, but in his mind, she's a loser. "She may have been able to steal the nomination from Bernie but she won't steal this election from me."

The press wants to know when they can expect to see Trump again. When he does make his next appearance, Trump plans to be complimentary of the other candidates. He'll congratulate both Clinton and Johnson for running strong campaigns, but will focus on his advantage in the Electoral College. His team is now giving him a crash course on the 12th Amendment. Trump's play for the presidency must not feel like a power grab. He's not stealing the presidency, he's merely a defender of the Constitution. The Constitution dictates that the election now go to the House of Representatives. He must emphasize this, and his surrogates must emphasize this at every turn. Clinton's people are already suggesting that the popular vote, not the Electoral College or Congress, should determine the next president. Trump must defend the Constitution. That's his path to the presidency.

Newt Gingrich can explain it. Newt is usually the smartest guy in any room, and he knows it. Newt used to be a college professor, and now the professor is on every cable news channel explaining the 12th Amendment. "Hillary can't try to steal the presidency by the fact that she won the popular vote," Gingrich explains. "That would be equivalent of changing the rules in the middle of the game, and we all should have learned as kids that we don't do that. Both Donald Trump and Hillary Clinton knew the rules of the game -- the rules of the election. The rules say the person with a majority of votes in the Electoral College wins. Not popular vote. Both Donald Trump and Hillary Clinton were competing to win states. By winning the popular vote, Hillary won a meaningless race. If she was seeking strategically to win the popular vote that was a very flawed strategy to win the presidency because you do not win the presidency by winning the popular vote."

The old professor is warming up. "Because neither candidate received a majority of electoral votes, the election will now go to the House of Representatives." Notice how Gingrich still only refers to the two major party candidates. Johnson's not in the club. That Mitt Romney, who Gingrich hates, is now meeting with Johnson, seals his disdain for the third party renegade.

"The Electoral College will meet on December 19th to actually cast their ballots for president. Look, Donald Trump is, right now, only one vote short of the necessary

270 votes. It's possible that an elector could change their mind. There is precedent for this and an elector currently committed to another candidate may decide that it's best for our country to expedite this process to vote for Donald Trump. Only one elector needs to do so. Only one elector would need to exercise their ability to vote for Donald Trump when the Electoral College meets on December 19th. Short of that happening, the 12th Amendment then stipulates that the election go to the House of Representatives. These are the rules of the election, established by the Constitution, that both candidates knew when they started this race. For Hillary's supporters to talk about the popular vote as if winning the popular vote gives her some right to the presidency, that's just poppycock."

Newt is the professor and all of Trump's surrogates are his students. They will use the same lines over and over again every time they are on TV. Clinton can't change the rules of the game. Trump is playing by the rules. Don't let Hillary Clinton change the rules. The Clinton's never think the rules apply to them. This time, the American people must hold the Clinton's accountable. The American people will not let Hillary Clinton change the rules so she can become president. The American people will make her play by the rules.

Newt says it first, then the surrogates say it, then the 38 million people who voted for Trump start saying it, and pretty soon even some of the Hillary Clinton people are saying it.

And Gary Johnson is just fine with that.

CHAPTER 7

Gary Johnson is content to lay low for a few weeks. Newt Gingrich is doing a fine job of explaining the 12th Amendment and the process of electing a president should the Electoral College fail to produce a winner.

When Gary Johnson gave his victory speech after winning New Mexico there were barely any members of the national media in attendance. The next day, when Mitt Romney came to town to endorse Johnson, there was a fever pitch around the Johnson campaign. Slowly, the press corps following Gary Johnson around has dwindled. A few commentators on cable news lay out elaborate scenarios where, should the stars align, Gary Johnson could theoretically win in the House. Johnson's supporters are growing, though. Mitt Romney is making the rounds. RNC Chairman Reince Priebus says Romney's got tinfoil on his head.

Imagine signing up to run a marathon, which is exactly 26.219 miles. Imagine how ready you would be to finish the race when you were at 26.1 miles. But the finish line pulls you in, and although you are completely exhausted, you now have the energy to finish the race. Then imagine that when you are at 26.218 miles, you're informed that the finish line has been moved and you must run several more miles.

This is what has just happened in the presidential election. Campaigns are grueling. Go into any campaign headquarters and there is always a sign up with the number of days until election. That sign is not just about creating urgency for the campaign. It is a sign telling everyone in the campaign how many days it is until they can sleep again.

Speaker Paul Ryan has urged the candidates and the campaigns to take a step back. The process will play out, he tells them. This advice is, of course, readily ignored.

Then there's Gary Johnson, who seems as relaxed as the Dalai Lama. "But still. Do not confuse his Zen-like quality for a lack of cojones. The guy has brass ones. " Lisa DePaulo wrote about Johnson in a GQ Magazine piece in 2011 that has been making the rounds on social media since election night. "He's a five-time Ironman triathlete. He paraglides and hot-gas balloons. (Not hot air, hot gas.) He biked across the Alps. And from the right angle, he looks like Harrison Ford."

Campaigns and marathons have at least one thing in common: they are both grueling. And unlike his opponents, Johnson has run a few marathons. Actually,

Johnson once competed in the epic 100-mile race at Leadville and completed the race in 29 hours, 45 minutes, and 9 seconds. He's climbed the tallest mountain on every continent, including Mount Everest. As the calendar turns to December, Johnson seems undeterred by a political mountain as big as Everest. He just keeps putting one foot in front of the other.

Newt Gingrich and the Trump surrogates have done their job. The country seems settled on the fact that barring a surprise in how the Electoral College votes on December 19, the House of Representatives will elect the next president.

The debate now seems to be focused on how exactly the state delegations should and will vote. Do congressional delegations in states that Clinton won have an obligation to vote for Clinton, even if Republicans have a majority of the congressional seats in that state? In this scenario, Trump narrowly wins the presidency, having won twenty-seven states on election night. Hillary won just twenty-two states and the District of Columbia, which does not get a vote in the House. Gary Johnson, of course, won just one state. This scenario is unlikely, pundits say. Clinton will not advocate for it because it leaves her four votes shy of the presidency without Trump voting states joining her, which goes again the premise of congressional delegations following the lead of voters on election night.

Trump will not argue that state congressional delegations follow the lead of voters in their states because Trump's better option is to convince Republicans to stay unified and vote along party lines. If every Republican in the House votes for Trump, Trump will win on a first ballot in the House with 31 votes.

The more you look at the facts -- the more you study the actual members of Congress who will be voting for the next president -- the easier it is to see why Donald Trump is acting like he is already the next President of the United States. Ben Carson does not seem crazy for hiring a real estate agent to find him a new home in Georgetown.

And then something happens.

CHAPTER 8

Monday, December 5, 2016

"CNN is reporting that the Gary Johnson campaign has called a press conference for 11 AM EST. We are told that this is a major announcement. In addition to Governor Johnson, we are told that Johnson's running mate Governor Bill Weld will be at the press conference as well as former Republican presidential candidate Mitt Romney. Other elected officials will be on hand, but we have not been told who those individuals are."

There's a buzz around the Johnson campaign. Johnson, Weld, and Romney all made the rounds on the Sunday talk shows and each hinted that something big was coming.

#TeamGov, as they like to call themselves, has been making the rounds. After their high profile meeting near Santa Fe the day after the election, a reporter asked Johnson where he was going next. "South Dakota," was his answer, and it wasn't to see Mount Rushmore. Johnson and Romney were meeting with Congresswoman Kristi

Noem, a Republican with a bit of a libertarian streak, who was a vocal critic of Trump throughout his campaign. Noem is South Dakota's lone congressional representative. All they had to do was convince one person to get behind Johnson and that would equal one vote toward twenty-six in the House.

From South Dakota they were onto Nebraska where two out of three congressional representatives in the House are Republicans and both had very serious reservations about supporting Trump. Nebraska Senator Ben Sasse, though not a member of the House, is one of the most influential Republicans in the state and was on record saying he would never support Donald Trump. The #NeverTrump winds in Nebraska were strong. All Johnson had to do was convince two people to back him, and that was another vote toward twenty-six in the House.

Then they were off to Idaho, where the state's only two members of Congress were both Republicans and both squeamish in their support for Trump. Raúl Labrador and Mike Simpson were more than happy to take a meeting with Governor Johnson when Mitt called.

The next stop was Alaska where #TeamGov met with Alaska's lone congressman and the third most senior member of the House of Representatives, Don Young. The fiery, freewheeling congressman was on record saying that Trump rode the wave of a bunch of idiots to the Republican nomination.

Utah Congressman Chris Stewart once referred to Donald Trump as "our Mussolini." Congresswoman Mia Love skipped the Republican National Convention for Trump's nomination. Congressman Rob Bishop was reluctant in his support of Trump. With Romney's influence in Utah and only four congressional representatives, all Republicans, Utah seemed like a good place to stop before heading back to New Mexico.

And at 11 AM EST on Monday, December 5th, Gary Johnson, Bill Weld, and Mitt Romney strolled into the conference room at the National Press Club in Washington with these nine members of Congress. These nine congressional representatives, representing a majority of the congressional delegations in their five respective states, were all declaring their intention to vote for Gary Johnson for President of the United States.

Gary Johnson spoke briefly about his meetings with each of the members of Congress and thanked them for their support. Then, one by one, each member of Congress spoke about why they were supporting Gary Johnson. Governor Bill Weld spoke and announced a series of town halls across the country. Gary wanted to tour the country and give the people a chance to get to know him better. He hoped that after they got to know him, and knowing now that they truly did have another option besides Clinton or Trump, that they would call their representatives and urge them to vote for him in the

House. Each of the nine members of Congress who were endorsing Gary Johnson today would be hosting town halls in their districts in the next few weeks, but they were scheduling additional town halls across the country.

Bill Weld spoke of the process outlined in the 12th Amendment, which Newt Gingrich had so finely educated the American public about over the past few weeks since the election. Romney reminded the members of the press that John Quincy Adams was elected president by the House of Representatives despite not winning the popular vote or leading in the Electoral College vote.

Donald Trump just went from thirty-one votes in the House to twenty-six. Still enough to win the presidency, but just by the skin of his teeth and the vote in the House is still over a month away.

At the National Press Club, it's pointed out by one reporter that Gary Johnson now appears to have five states, well short of twenty-six, and that the one state that actually voted for him, his home state of New Mexico, is absent from the stage.

"The New Mexico delegation is currently divided between Clinton and Trump. We have asked to meet with all three representatives from New Mexico; Michelle Lujan Grisham, Steve Pearch, and Ben Luján. So far, we've not been able to sit down with any of them, but I hope we'll have an opportunity to do so soon, and I'd encourage the voters of New Mexico to call these representatives and ask them to meet with me," Johnson said. "We have a long way to go, but I've climbed mountains before."

Reporters press Johnson on what states they'll be targeting next. "I am going to see a lot of this country between now and the first week of January, I'll tell you that," Johnson replied. "I'm sure Donald Trump and Hillary Clinton would love for me to tell you what members of Congress we're talking to next. But we're betting that this announcement today has turned some heads, and when I leave here I'm going to be making some phone calls."

Johnson speaks so freely, so casually. He just mentioned he's going to make some phone calls, so now, of course, the press wants to know who he's calling.

"You may have heard my plans if I don't win the election. I'm planning to Ride the Divide this summer. It's a 2,700 mile bike ride along the Continental Divide that runs through the United States. It actually starts in Canada and ends at the US-Mexican border." And with a smile Johnson adds, "I have a hotel reservation up in Canada for the week before the race starts. I think I need to call and cancel my reservation."

CHAPTER 9

Donald Trump has made a potentially fatal error. Throughout his campaign he ran away from the Republican Party. Rather than reaching out and trying to build partnerships, he repeatedly said that he would win on his own. After election night when it became clear the election would go to the House of Representatives, Trump took Republican support for granted. Now, nine Republican congressional representatives have defected to support Gary Johnson.

Trump responds as Trump responds. He isolates. Don Young is a little kooky, he says. Kristi Noem isn't a serious person, Trump contends. She's from South Dakota. We can't let one not serious representative from a small state manipulate the system and circumvent the will of the millions of people in other states. Since Trump declared his candidacy he has been saying the system is rigged. This is proof. This is the ultimate in ugly, establishment politics.

Trump's supporters are enraged. Their anger is near a boiling point, and Trump is turning them loose on the defected congressmen. Trump goes to Lincoln, Nebraska to hold a rally and outside his supporters burn in effigy representatives Jeff Fortenberry and Adrian Smith, who have pledged their support to Johnson.

Johnson's town halls turn chaotic. Wherever Johnson goes, Trump supporters are outside protesting. Gingrich and the Trump surrogates warn that these defecting Republicans are running the risk of giving the presidency to Clinton. Each of the nine defecting Republicans are under immense pressure. The party warns them that money is going to dry up. Now it's a race against time. Johnson must get more representatives on board to keep the momentum going before the pressure builds and one of his nine turns back to Trump.

Meanwhile, Clinton, along with the Democratic machine, is trying to figure out how to move beyond seventeen, the number of states with Democrat controlled delegations. No Republican will ever vote for her. Never. But there are now nine Republicans who have come out for Johnson, and this is Clinton's window of opportunity.

The Democrats picked up a congressional seat in Nevada on election night, and now the Nevada congressional delegation is evenly split with two Republicans and two Democrats. They must convince one of the Republicans to vote for Johnson. If they can do that, Clinton will take Nevada. They will deploy the same strategy in all states where congressional delegations are closely divided. The morning after the election, when Clinton was close to coming unglued, she realized that she needed Johnson. Gary Johnson has done exactly what she needed him to do. He has built his own momentum, now she will help him. It's a risky move, but it's the only move she's got.

Democrats picked up a seat in Virginia on election night and the congressional delegation is divided five Republicans to four Democrats. Clinton won Virginia, just like she won Nevada. They need to get two Republicans in Virginia to back Johnson. If they can do that, Hillary will take Virginia.

Next they'll target Arizona, where the delegation is split five Republicans to four Democrats. And then on to Wisconsin where it's five Republicans to three Democrats, but Clinton won Wisconsin providing weight for her argument.

If the Hillary Clinton camp can fuel the Johnson flames in Nevada, Virginia, Arizona, and Wisconsin, she will move from 17 to 21. By fanning the Johnson flames, Hillary builds her own momentum, and there's a name on the board for Clinton's big bombshell.

Politicians are masters at surviving. This is their primary objective. Survive and advance. There are few hills politicians are willing to die on. Longtime Clinton insider John Podesta has a plan. They draw up a list of every Republican in the House serving in districts that traditionally vote Democratic. These representatives know their tenures in Congress are likely to be short lived. But Clinton can guarantee them a future in politics; a cabinet position, an appointment, an ambassadorship with a house in Spain.

The Maine congressional delegation is evenly divided with one Republican and one Democrat. The Republican, Bruce Poliquin, from Maine's 2nd Congressional district, just won re-election for a second term by the thinnest of margins. His district went for Clinton, though, and has gone for every Democratic candidate for President since Bill Clinton in 1992. How many more elections before Poliquin's luck runs out? Maybe Poliquin needs a house in Spain.

That will get Clinton to twenty-two, and she'll have picked up a state by getting someone to vote for her. And not just anyone, a Republican. This is the moment that Hillary Clinton needs. That's when she makes her move.

"Johnson can't waste a day because he has so much ground to cover." Clinton's strategist Joel Benenson is beginning to see their path to the White House. It's a narrow one, but he can see it. "Let's lay the groundwork and get our people on board, but we won't announce anything until after January 1. You see what's happening with the Johnson Nine now. Those nine reps are getting slaughtered. We need to get our people to hold off going public in order to limit their exposure. The new Congress is not even seated until January 3rd. The earliest we could have a first vote in the House is the 6th. That's the day the votes from the Electoral College are officially counted. All we need to do is make sure Trump does not have enough votes to win on a first ballot."

James Carville is now at Hillary Clinton's campaign headquarters. Carville and the Clinton's go way back. He was Bill Clinton's top strategist when Bill Clinton beat George Bush in 1992. He's brilliant and ruthless. It's just he and Podesta now.

"These Republicans in Nevada, Arizona, Virginia, Wisconsin," Carville starts, "They know that at this point a vote for Johnson is a vote for Hillary Clinton. And their districts know it. We've got to be ready to give them parachutes."

"I don't know how we're going to do this," Podesta responds. "Everything is already promised. Cabinet positions, appointments. Everything."

"So we double promise. Hell, we triple promise." James Carville is a very practical person. "It's the economy, stupid," was his line in 1992 that encapsulated the entire campaign. "If you have to promise the same cabinet position to three different people to make sure you win the presidency, that's what you do."

"Hell, this is fun, John," Carville continues. "I've never had so much fun. Even in '92 when we were riding the wave and it was clear we had it, I'm having more fun now than I had then. This is better than sex."

"And Hillary is kicking ass out there. I've never seen her this good. And we've got the public on our side. She won the popular vote. More people voted for her than voted for anyone else. So what if people find out we're selling off cabinet positions to win this thing."

"We're holding off until after January 1 for our people to go public," Podesta says. "But we're not dealing with a stagnant situation here. What's Trump offering people? Are they over there doing the same thing; getting their ducks in a row to announce on the 3rd or the 4th of the 6th that they have 26 votes?"

"That's what's scary about this -- and what makes it so much Goddamn fun," Carville jumps in. "We can't trust anyone. We get a Republican in Arizona to tell us he's voting for Johnson. He may be playing us. Maybe Trump's already promised to make him Defense Secretary when we're offering him to be the Ambassador to Timbuktu. So we've got to get this thing fucking air tight."

Clinton's people have a strategy to get her to 22. Trump will be at 23 votes and Johnson at five votes. Maybe Johnson will pick off a few more states. Maybe Johnson will be at seven and Trump at 22. Then Clinton would be in the lead. Maybe Johnson picks up five more and Trump is at 18.

"It would be good to be in the lead," Podesta says, "but we don't want Johnson picking up too much support. We've got to fan the flames, but also control them."

It's dangerous playing with fire.

CHAPTER 10

December 26, 2017

"They're going to target Nevada and Maine. They need to win those states first, that's got to be their strategy." Trump's campaign manager, Paul Manafort, is standing in front of a map of the United States. It's been 21 days since the number of Red States dropped from 31 to 26. Seventeen states are marked Blue for Hillary Clinton. Five have been marked Black for Gary Johnson. Manafort chose Black to show his disgust for the Johnson Nine. Two are marked purple, Nevada and Maine, where the state delegations are evenly split between Republicans and Democrats.

Manafort scans a list of representatives from Nevada and Maine; a list of names he's sure Hillary's people are also surveying.

"I want to know everything there is to know about this Bruce Poliquin. What are his hot button issues? Who's funded his campaigns? Look at his investments. Look into the investment firm where he used to work."

Paul Manafort is a political veteran. His resume goes all the way back to Gerald Ford and along the way he's worked for Reagan, George H.W. Bush, Bob Dole, and John McCain. When not working for aspiring presidents, he's a lobbyist by trade, and one of Washington's most powerful. His clients are not always the most upstanding, but the money is good.

If the people at Trump's rallies knew the biography of the person running his campaign, they might be less sure of Trump as the standard bearer of the anti-establishment. Manafort built the Republican establishment while building a personal fortune representing some of the world's most dubious figures. Manafort's racket for more than three decades has been to turn dictators into freedom fighters. Jonas Savimbi was the leader of the violent Angolan rebel group UNITA. Savimbi paid Manafort $600,000 and it was money well spent. Despite his Maoist background, Savimbi was suddenly the darling of the Reagan Administration. The conservative Heritage Foundation hosted a reception for Savimbi, who was taking a break from his war crimes to tour Washington, and introduced as a "linguist, philosopher, poet, politician, warrior … one of the few authentic heroes of our time."

In the 1980's Manafort received payments of $900,000 a year from Philippine dictator Ferdinand Marcos. He also lobbied for Siad Barre of Somalia and Mobutu Sese Seko of Zaïre. Other clients included the governments of the Dominican Republic, Equatorial Guinea, Kenya, and Nigeria. In 1992, in a report from The Center for Public Integrity by Pamela Brogan, Manafort was named part of what was called "The Torturer's Lobby."

He was paid under the table by a Lebanese arms dealer for his involvement in French elections and $700,000 by Pakistan intelligence agency for covert actions where he posed as a CNN reporter. He's even dabbled in Ukrainian politics, where he worked as an advisor to Viktor Yanukovych, who has close ties to Russia's Vladimir Putin.

It's nice work if you can get it. Help elect a president and then lobby that president for aid on behalf of your clients. Without Manafort, Savimbi was just another militant guerilla. Thanks to Manafort's connections to the Reagan White House, Congress would send hundreds of millions of dollars to Savimbi's UNITA. Savimbi and the other questionable characters who hire Manafort are very smart. It's a small investment with a big payoff.

"Manafort and Stone [Manafort's former partner] pioneered a new style of firm, what K Street would come to call a double-breasted operation," Franklin Foer wrote for Slate shortly after Manafort joined the Trump campaign. "One wing of the shop managed campaigns, electing a generation of Republicans, from Phil Gramm to Arlen Specter. The other wing lobbied the officials they helped to victory on behalf of its corporate clients."

Donald Trump trusts Paul Manafort completely. The two have done battle together before. Trump first hired Manafort's firm in the early 90's to help him stop the proliferation of Indian casinos, which would cut into Trump's Atlantic City interests. Trump was even called to testify before Congress where he said, "Nobody likes Indians as much as Donald Trump. There is no way Indians are going to protect themselves from the mob ... It will be the biggest scandal ever, the biggest since Al Capone ... An Indian chief is going to tell Joey Killer to please get off his reservation? It's unbelievable to me."

But New York Governor George Pataki, a Republican, eventually fined Trump $250,000 and demanded he publicly apologize for running a smear campaign against his potential Indian competitors. "Manafort didn't own the Trump account at the firm," Foer wrote for Slate, "But one of his former partners told me that he would dispense advice and pitch in, winning Trump's trust. When Manafort took an apartment in Trump Towers in 2006, he would kibitz with his old client when they'd run into one another on the elevator."

Manafort hasn't decided what he'll do yet once Trump becomes president. Of course, he could go with Trump to the White House, and he and Trump have discussed various roles he could fill. Manafort could also go back to K Street, and with Trump in the White House clients would be beating down his door. He could make millions;

enough money to make the rumored duffel bags of cash from Ferdinand Marcos look like chump change.

Whichever he chooses, Manafort stands to win big with a Trump win. This congressman from Maine -- Bruce Poliquin -- who Paul Manafort had never heard of until a few weeks ago, is one guy who could screw things up for him big time.

"Get Poliquin in here," Manafort barks. "Before he gets here, I want to know every piece of dirt on him. Who's he fucked? I want to know everything about this guy."

The next day staffers arrive with the bad news. Bruce Poliquin, by all accounts, is a nice guy. How else does a Republican win a solidly Democratic district in the state of Maine?

On his website, Poliquin introduces himself saying, "I'm a third generation Central Mainer from a big-hearted Franco-American family. I grew up in central Maine, studied in the public schools, and worshipped at Sacred Heart Church. I was raised with a deep respect for the honest, hard-working people of Maine."

His father was a teacher, coach, and principal. Poliquin worked his way through college doing grunt work and eventually made a few million bucks working in Chicago and New York City before returning home to Maine to start a family with his wife. When he was 39-years-old, he was on a family vacation at a resort in Puerto Rico when he wife got caught up in a bad current swimming off the coast and drowned. Poliquin became a single dad to their 16-month old son. By all appearances he was a great dad. He coached Little League baseball before getting into politics.

"Well, shit," Manafort said with resignation. "This is going to be harder than I thought."

The next day Poliquin is at Trump Headquarters with Donald Trump and Paul Manafort. They're schmoozing, but walking a fine line. They've got to have this guy, but at the same time they do not want to appear desperate.

Poliquin assures them that Donald Trump has his support. How can they know for sure? During his own tight re-election campaign, Poliquin ran away from Trump. Publicly he gave only a tacit endorsement. Bruce Poliquin doesn't seem like a guy ready to hitch his wagon to the Trump train. Is Bruce Poliquin really going to take an appointment from Donald Trump? If Poliquin plays his cards right, he could end up being governor. Getting too cozy with Trump seems a risky move.

Manafort makes all of these calculations intuitively. He understands it's good to bring in Poliquin and make him feel important. This meeting is about making sure their base is solid. They're not going to take anyone for granted anymore, not after the defections of the Johnson Nine.

They don't want to draw attention to Poliquin, or remind the voters of Maine's 2nd congressional district, who overwhelmingly voted for Hillary Clinton, that in the House Bruce Poliquin will cast his vote for Donald Trump. Manafort feels good. "Bruce is a reliable vote. Let's not draw attention to him and expose him."

Bruce Poliquin will vote for Trump and Democrat Chellie Pingree from Maine's 1st District will vote for Hillary Clinton and their votes will cancel one another out. Team Trump feels confident. Over the next two days they're meeting with the Republican representatives from each of the 26 states he's counting on in the House. They're determined to not lose one more vote. The meeting with Poliquin was really about making sure Hillary didn't pick off anyone. They were taking the House Republicans for granted before. They won't make that mistake again.

Johnson showed his hand too soon. Hillary Clinton is weak. Team Trump is a unified force moving toward New Year's Day.

CHAPTER 11

The big question is what really happened on December 19. On December 19th the Electoral College met in all 50 states and the District of Columbia to officially cast their ballots for president.

On election night Donald Trump won 269 electoral votes, only one shy of securing the presidency. While feeling confident of their plan to secure the presidency in the House of Representatives, the Trump campaign was also working behind the scenes to keep the election from going to the House at all. All Donald Trump needed was for one elector to break rank and vote for him instead of Hillary Clinton or Gary Johnson.

Hillary Clinton and Gary Johnson know this, and they too have worked diligently to ensure that all of their pledged electors hold the line. All the campaigns have actually gone a step further with everyone trying to pick off as many electors as possible.

In past elections, nobody's ever known the names of electors, and the process of the electors actually casting their ballots for president and vice president on the second Wednesday of December has gone mainly unnoticed. That wasn't at all the case this year. Reporters hounded electors and Democratic and Republican officials wined and dined pledged electors in an effort to ensure nobody broke rank.

Electors in the Electoral College are party people. These are political junkies who have come up in their parties and have further ambitions within their parties. For an elector to defect and vote for a candidate outside of their party goes against the nature of most of them.

Yet some Republicans in the House -- the Johnson Nine --have already demonstrated a willingness to break party rank. Could Republican electors pledged to Donald Trump also break rank to vote for Gary Johnson?

In 1972, Roger MacBride, an elector from Virginia pledged to vote for Richard Nixon for president and Spiro Agnew for vice-president, instead he cast his electoral votes for Libertarian candidates John Hospers and Theodora Nathan. That vote cast for Theodora Nathan was the first vote cast for a woman in the history of the Electoral College. Four years earlier a North Carolina elector, who was pledged to vote for Nixon, instead voted for segregationist George Wallace. There were more instances, mainly to garner personal attention, and others that were likely outright mistakes.

With only a handful of examples in U.S. history of electors' ever breaking rank, it seemed far-fetched that Hillary Clinton would be able to pick up the needed six electoral votes in order to win the presidency. If the Electoral College were to decide the presidency, it seemed that it would be the result of a Hillary Clinton or Gary Johnson elector defecting to Trump. But now that December 19 has passed, with the votes sealed until January 6, all the campaigns can do is proceed while assuming that the electors voted as pledged until the votes are officially counted in a Joint Session of Congress on January 6 with the result mirroring that of election night.

Donald Trump is working the Republican Congressional Delegation. Speaker Paul Ryan has become his new best friend. Ryan, though not a Trump fan, sees a legislative ally in Trump. Ryan has a good relationship with Trump's vice presidential running mate Mike Pence built when the two served in Congress together. Pence will have far reaching authority in the Trump White House and will work with Congress on both foreign and domestic policy. Trump's temperament bothers Paul Ryan, but if Ryan can work with Pence to advance a legislative agenda that Trump will sign off on, Paul Ryan is willing to whip up votes for Trump in Congress.

First, they have to get Pence elected vice-president. In order to be elected vice-president, Pence must receive

51 votes in the Senate. There are 51 Republicans in the Senate, but a few moderates are non-committal so far. He has 49 committed votes in the Senate. Tim Kaine, the Democratic nominee for vice-president, has 49 committed votes, with every Democrat and the two independents in the Senate who caucus with the Democrats all supporting Kaine.

If Tim Kaine becomes vice-president under Donald Trump, he will be relegated to ultimate outsider status. John Adams, who served as vice president under George Washington, considered the vice presidency the most boring job known to man. If the Senate elects Kaine as vice-president, Trump will make his job even more boring. The Trump Administration will have to find another place for Pence. His job title may change, but his job description will remain the same.

In the final days of 2016, Barack Obama stumps endlessly for Hillary Clinton. All of his criticism is directed towards Donald Trump. He extends kind words towards Gary Johnson referring to Hillary Clinton and Gary Johnson as being two reasonable candidates for the House to consider. Of course, he is supporting Hillary, Obama tells the crowds, but he can understand how a reasonable person might support Gary Johnson. But Donald Trump, Obama warns, is dangerous. Barack Obama declares he knows what it takes to be president and Donald Trump is not fit to be president.

On New Year's Eve Trump holds a rally in Washington, D.C. It's almost a pre-inaugural party. He will make America great again. He will make America safe again. Crooked Hillary belongs in jail, and one speaker even threatens that if she tries to steal the White House there will be riots in Washington.

Hillary's people have been quietly making calls. Democrats are a unified force, but so far they've been unable to persuade any Republicans in closely split states to defect to Johnson. Her campaign had hoped to come out , perhaps even on New Year's Day, and announce that they had picked up a few votes; instead, they're stuck. Johnson likewise is stuck as well as the calendar prepares to turn to 2017 and a potential first vote in the House less than a week away. Donald Trump is still holding onto 26 votes in the House; just the number of votes he needs to secure the presidency.

CHAPTER 12

On January 3, 2017 the newly elected House of Representatives is officially seated. The 435 members of Congress are divided 234 Republicans to 201 Democrats, but more importantly, Republicans control the state delegations of 31 States. Thanks to the Johnson Nine, five of those 31 states are poised to vote for Gary Johnson, but Trump still has the 26 votes necessary to become the next President of the United States on a first ballot in the House.

It's now January 6 and a Joint Session of Congress is ready to officially count the electoral votes for president and vice president of the United States. At 1:00 PM, the President of the Senate, Vice President Joe Biden, opens the session. Biden is at the podium with Speaker of the House Paul Ryan. It is Biden who is officially presiding and he sits in the chair normally reserved for the Speaker of the House.

The chamber doors open and two Senate pages carrying two mahogany boxes enter. These two mahogany boxes contain the certified vote from all fifty states and the District of Columbia. The boxes are placed on two tables before the Congress. The House and Senate select two members each to read the votes. Normally, each House of Congress will select one Republican and one Democrat, but this time, the selection is more thoughtful. Alaska Congressman Don Young is the longest tenured Republican in the House, but he has been chosen due to his support for Gary Johnson. Democratic Congressman John Conyers, the longest serving member of the House of Representatives, who supported Hillary Clinton, is also chosen from the House. Senator Jeff Sessions, the first United States Senator to endorse Donald Trump, is chosen from the Senate along with Senator Angus King, an Independent from Maine.

The votes are read and tallied without objection. Vice President Joe Biden announces the results.

The results are: 268 Trump, 264 Hillary, 6 Gary Johnson. Baoky Vu, an elector from the state of Georgia, became a faithless elector and voted for Gary Johnson instead of Donald Trump to whom the elector was pledged to.

In the vice-presidential race the results are: 269 Pence, 264 Kaine, 5 Bill Weld. Vu casts his electoral vote for Pence as pledged.

With the official tally of the Electoral College votes, the election of the next President of the United States officially moves to the United States House of Representatives and the election of the next Vice President of the United States officially moves to the United States Senate. The Senate departs the House Chamber to return to the Senate Chamber. In accordance with the 12th amendment of the United States Constitution, voting will take place immediately.

"This is our last chance, John. This is it."

It's the afternoon of January 5, the day prior to the official counting of the electoral votes. If no candidate hits 270, Speaker Paul Ryan has indicated that the next item of business in the House will be to elect a president. Senate Majority Leader Mitch McConnell has indicated that the Senate, likewise, is ready to elect the vice-president.

Hillary has been unable to get any traction and is stuck at 17 states. There is depression in the air at Hillary Clinton headquarters, not so much because it appears Trump will win, but because they have not been able to move the needle at all. The Trump campaign cannot wait for tomorrow. The Johnson campaign meanwhile is frantically working.

"Tomorrow morning, Donald Trump is going to be elected president, John. You said not supporting him was a matter of conscious. Then how can you in good conscious do nothing while the man gets elected?"

"The Libertarians in this state hate me, Mitt."

Mitt Romney is on the phone with another governor, trying to add a fourth governor to #TeanGov. Ohio Governor John Kasich, the last man standing in the Republican primary before finally succumbing to Donald Trump, is trying to fend off Romney's request to put together a last minute meeting of the Republican members of the Ohio Congressional delegation.

John Kasich was elected Governor of Ohio with a bit of a power play, using party influence of the Republican juggernaut to stave off a Libertarian insurgency.

"Who cares if the Libertarians in your state hate you? This is about doing the right thing. Besides, if you do this, they'll love you for it." If Mitt Romney is going to convince John Kasich to put together a meeting before tomorrow's vote, he has to do so right now.

There's a long pause on the phone.

"John, I felt sick when I woke up the morning after the election. I'd voted for Gary, but I couldn't help but wonder how much more he could have accomplished on election night if I'd been public with my support. Maybe this wouldn't have been such an uphill battle."

"He's at five votes, Mitt. He's a long way off. Even if we get Ohio, he's a long way off." It doesn't escape Romney's attention that Governor Kasich just referred to the Johnson campaign as *we*.

"We don't have to get Gary to 26 tomorrow. We just have to get Trump down to 25. One day at a time. Help us, John. I'm telling you, I'm speaking to you as a friend. If you're inclined to do this and you don't because you're hedging for some political reason, you are going to watch Donald Trump get elected president tomorrow. And John, just as I felt sick the morning after the election, you are going to feel even sicker. You are going to be disgusted with yourself because you're going to know that you perhaps had the power to keep that man from becoming president and you did nothing. The only thing necessary for the triumph of evil is for good men to do nothing."

Another long pause.

"I'm in."

"Alright, John," that's fantastic."

"We don't have a moment to spare," Kasich replies. He was careful in his deliberations, but now that his mind is made up he is thinking and talking fast.

I'm going to hang up the phone and start making calls immediately. I'll alert my detail. I can be on my way to Washington in 30 minutes. Before I leave, I'll have gotten on the phone with every Republican House member from Ohio."

"I gotta warn you, Mitt. These guys are their own men.

They're not going to get pushed around by you, me, or anyone."

"We're not going to try to push anyone around, John, but you know the party there. You can assure these guys that if they stand with us that you'll stand with them, right? They need to know they're not going to get hung out to dry."

"Absolutely. I'll call you when I get to Washington." As Romney hangs up the phone, a twinkle appears in his eye as he considers that perhaps they can stop Trump afterall.

At 9 PM on January 5 Governors Gary Johnson, Bill Weld, Mitt Romney, and John Kasich convene with the Republican members of the Ohio Congressional delegation in Romney's suite at the Ritz Carlton in Pentagon City, just outside of Washington.

Kasich opens the meeting. He speaks from the heart about why he decided he could never vote for Donald Trump. He talks about the Republican National Convention being in Cleveland and the pressure to come out and endorse and the depths he had to reach within his own heart and soul to remain true to himself.

"A few days before the Convention, Donald Trump, Jr. came to me," Kasich says. "You could be the most powerful vice-president in the history of our country. Foreign policy, domestic policy; you'll set the agenda. I got to tell you, it really was hard resisting the pressure to endorse up to that point, but as I considered what was being presented, I felt like there I was about to make a deal with the devil."

"Tomorrow, we can elect a president or we can choose to not elect a president;" Romney's got the floor now. "If there's any doubt in your mind, we should not. If there's any thought in your mind that maybe Donald Trump is not the right man to be president, if you have even the slightest hesitation shouldn't we push pause? You guys voting for Gary Johnson tomorrow doesn't make Gary president. It just pushes pause."

Why does Ohio always seem to be at the center of presidential elections? It was the state that put Bush over the top in his 2004 re-election campaign. Bush won Ohio by just 2.1 percent and it was Ohio's 20 electoral votes that pushed him over 270 electoral votes. If John Kerry had won Ohio, John Kerry would have been president. If Hillary had won Ohio, she would now be just a few days away from being inaugurated as the 45th President of the United States. Ohio went for Obama in 2008 and 2012, but for some reason, in close elections, Ohio just does not like Democrats.

As Ohio goes, so goes the nation. For the second time in this election, Ohio is in a position to grant, or not grant the presidency. Ohio could have given Hillary Clinton the presidency on election night, and it didn't. Tomorrow, in the House, the Ohio Congressional delegation can cast it's vote for Donald J. Trump and in so doing they will elect Trump as the 45th President of the United States. Or they can say "hold on a minute" and push pause by voting for Johnson.

Republicans lost one Ohio Congressional seats on election night, but still control a strong majority of the delegation with eleven Republicans to five Democrats. In reality, #TeamGov only needs to convince five of Ohio's Republicans to vote for Johnson. If they can do that, Trump and Johnson will be tied and Ohio will not cast a vote, dropping Trump to 25. John Kasich hasn't come this far, though, to broker a tie.

"C'mon, guys. What's it going to take?" Kasich asks almost rhetorically.

"You're asking us to sacrifice our careers," replies one of the congressmen.

Gary Johnson puts his finger in the air, calmly, to indicate he has something to say. "With all due respect, Congressman, we are not asking you to sacrifice your career. Serving in Congress was supposed to be the sacrifice. Build a life, build a business, build a career --

and then sacrifice those things so that you can serve your country. Build a life, and then lay that life down at the altar of your country. I suspect that when you first got into this, when you first got into politics and you first ran for office, it wasn't about your career in politics. That's who I'm appealing to today. But, if you guys are more worried about your political fortunes than you are your country, I'm afraid we're talking to the wrong group of people."

Silence.

One second, two seconds, three seconds. What feels like an eternity as the seconds tick away pass before John Kasich breaks the silence. "Gentlemen, most of you have been in Congress long enough to know that with rare exceptions, if you really want to have an impact, if you really want to be a player, you've got to stick around there for 20 years. Twenty years of pushing paper and carrying water. And you know how it goes. I've been there, man."

"You want to run for Congress again," Weld jumps in. "We'll help you. Run as a Republican or run as a Libertarian. Hell, run as a Unitarian. We'll help you. We'll be there for you. We'll help you raise money. And you can run knowing that you're actually serving your country, not yourself. Will the voters know that? I don't know. We'll have to find out. But you'll know it, and isn't that what matters?"

The governors have made their pitch, but none of the congressmen want to show their hand. "Here's what we're going to do guys," Kasich says as he takes the small notepad from next to the phone and begins tearing off pages and handing them to the congressmen. "We need to know, are you in or are you out, but we don't want to put anybody on the spot. So just take this piece of paper and write a single word – in or out. Are you in or are you out? Give the papers to me and I'll tally them up. If you are all out, I'll know that we don't need to continue talking. But, if four, or five, or six of you are in, let's keep talking."

Within a few moments the votes are in and Kasich tallies the numbers. Eight to three.

When one of the out votes realizes that eight of his colleagues are in, he switches and now; it's nine to two. The two congressmen who oppose say they'll never change their vote. They have to be true to their party and it's time for them to go. #TeamGov and the new Ohio Nine huddle and talk about the vote tomorrow. The Ohio delegation will go for Gary Johnson on a vote of nine for Gary Johnson, five for Hillary Clinton, and two for Donald Trump.

More importantly, Donald Trump just went to 25 votes in the House, one vote short of enough to become president.

CHAPTER 14

Hillary Clinton and Gary Johnson are absent from the Gallery of the House of Representatives, but Donald Trump wouldn't miss this moment for the world. He's surrounded by family and his closest friends and advisors confident he is about to be elected President of the United States. Paul Manafort is seated a row behind him just over his left shoulder. Adjacent to his right shoulder is Governor Mike Pence, who's joined by his family. News crews have a camera fixed on the Speaker's chair, the House Clerk, and the Trump passel.

Paul Ryan has now brought the House of Representatives to order. It's time to vote.

In a role such as this, Ryan has no interest in appearing to make a power play. He is simply presiding over the vote. He instructs House members on the process. The Clerk will call House members to the floor to cast their ballots. Members will be called by state with the states called alphabetically. Alabama, which is the first state alphabetically, will have its representatives called first. When all of the representatives from a state have been called, the Clerk will tally the votes from that state and one vote for president will be cast. So the first member of the House to be called will be the representative from Alabama's 1st Congressional District, then Alabama's 2nd Congressional District, and so forth until all of Alabama's congressional representatives have voted. When all of Alabama's representatives have voted, the Clerk will tally their votes and determine which candidate the State of Alabama is casting their lone majority vote for in the presidential contest. After Alabama, the Alaska delegation will follow and each state successively all the way through to Wyoming.

Alabama easily goes for Trump and then Congressman Don Young of Alaska gives his state's support to Gary Johnson. Next Arizona goes for Trump by a vote of five to four. Arkansas easily goes to Trump followed just as easily by California for Hillary. The next state to vote is Colorado where Republicans had held the advantage in the state congressional delegation until election night when the Democrats flipped a seat. Now the Democrats control the delegation by a margin of four to three. Gary Johnson campaigned heavily in Colorado and won almost 30 percent of the popular vote on election night. Since he began doing his town halls in early December, he has held eight in Colorado. Republican Scott Tipton from Colorado's 3rd Congressional District calls out the name Gary Johnson when he appears before the House Clerk to vote. Colorado goes for Hillary Clinton by a vote of four to Clinton, two for Trump, and one for Johnson.

The next five states to cast their votes are predictable. Connecticut and Delaware go for Clinton. Florida and Georgia go for Trump. Hawaii for Clinton. The next state to vote is Idaho and the two Idaho representatives, Raúl Labrador and Mike Simpson, both part of the original Johnson Nine, both cast their votes for Gary Johnson. Johnson now has two votes for president in the United States House of Representatives.

By the time Kevin Cramer, North Dakota's lone representative throws his state's support behind Donald Trump, the audience in the chamber and watching at home on television is falling into the rhythm of the proceedings. Things are going mostly as predicted. Trump, it seems, is on his way to the presidency.

Next up is Ohio. Steve Chabot of Ohio's 1st Congressional District turns heads when he votes for Gary Johnson, but he's not the first Republican to go rogue in the vote. When Brad Wenstrup from Ohio's 2nd Congressional District also votes for Johnson, commotion breaks out on the floor and in the gallery.

Paul Manafort leaves the gallery and is putting his phone up to his ear as he exits the camera view. There's a bustle on the House floor and Speaker Ryan bangs his gavel to quiet the crowd for the next representative to vote. Representative Joyce Beatty votes for Hillary Clinton as predicted. Trump gets a vote. Hillary gets another vote. Then a few more for Johnson. When the Ohio delegation has completed voting it's nine for Johnson, five for Clinton, and two for Trump.

The Trump party in the galley of the House Chamber is stone-faced as Oklahoma is called to vote. All five Oklahoma representatives vote for Trump and things are back on track.

South Dakota and Utah go for Johnson, as predicted, as the states are under control of part of the original Johnson Nine. 435 members from all 50 states have now voted and Paul Ryan announces the results: 25 states for Trump, 17 for Clinton, and 6 for Johnson with two states failing to cast a vote.

The House adjourns with no comment from the Speaker on when there will be another vote. When his gavel hits the table to adjourn the session, Trump and his team quickly leave the gallery and a flurry of action breaks out on the House floor. The original Johnson Nine are making their way to the Ohio Delegation as is the House Republican leadership.

With no second vote yet on the agenda, nobody knows how long they have to make a new deal, or to hold onto the deal they've already made. It's two weeks until Inauguration Day and we still don't know who will be the next president.

CHAPTER 15

The Senate returns to their Chamber without Vice President Joe Biden, who is on his way to the White House. Hillary Clinton's running mate, Senator Tim Kaine from Virginia, is well-liked by his colleagues. The Senate is divided 51 to 49 and the Democrats like their chances. Moderate Republicans have been hesitant to commit to Pence when there's a guy with a good smile who has a record of being tough on crime sitting right across the aisle from them. On the first ballot in the Senate the vote to elect the next vice-president, the Senate is deadlocked at 50-50.

The White House hastily announces an address from the Oval Office by President Obama for that evening at 7:00 PM EST now that the House and Senate have both failed to produce a president and vice-president. By the time the House was done voting there was less than an hour left before the markets closed for the weekend, but in a mere 50 minutes the Dow dropped 15%. Right-wing commentators speculate that Obama is on the verge of declaring martial law and blame the Ohio Nine. Donald Trump may be a flawed candidate, they reason, but he is far and away better than Hillary Clinton, and certainly much better than an indefinite Obama presidency through martial law.

Friday evening is typically a magical time. It's the time of the week when you let loose with the cares of the week behind you. On this Friday, however, there is a cloud of fear hanging over the country. Hillary Clinton's supporters have taken to the argument once again that she has a rightful claim to the presidency due to her popular vote plurality. The fact that Hillary has been magnificent on the campaign trail since election night has made the public more sympathetic towards her. Trump's supporters are asserting their will. Trump rode a wave of disenfranchised voters to the Republican nomination. If they are denied the presidency through political maneuvering, their rage just may boil over.

Paul Ryan has been summoned to the White House to meet with Obama prior to his Oval Office address. The two men are different in so many ways; different skin color, different upbringings, and different political views. Obama and Ryan also have some things in common. Both have been calming, soothing forces during this time of uncertainty for our nation. Neither has appeared interested in using this crisis as an opportunity to seize power or advance their own agendas.

At the White House, President Obama and Speaker Ryan discuss security. The FBI and Secret Service have been collaborating to assess credible threats. The United States Capitol Police is maintaining a security detail on Speaker Ryan and other House leadership, but their resources are stretched thin. In recent weeks, several House members who typically enjoy anonymity, have been targeted. Secret Service and FBI officials brief the President and Speaker on credible threats to the Johnson Nine. Since the vote in the House this afternoon they have also intercepted online communications and threats toward the Ohio Nine.

White House staff interrupt the meeting on several occasions. Obama interjects his thoughts on speech drafts and he gives instructions on the tone and feel of what he wants to communicate. In less than two weeks, he will be a former president, but right now he is presiding over a nation in doubt. Obama has long relished his role as counselor in chief. He is perhaps as well suited for this role as any president to ever face such a time as this.

With the reports submitted by the Secret Service and FBI, a plan is made. The Secret Service will provide additional resources to the Capitol Police. House members with credible threats will receive security details. Ryan and Capitol Police will be meeting later this evening with House members to discuss security details.

Ryan is about to be ushered out; Obama is scheduled to address the nation in less than 20 minutes and the president has yet to approve a final draft of his speech.

Ryan requests a moment of the president's time, alone.

Alone together, Ryan asks that the two men pray together.

"Our Father, who art in Heaven, hallowed be Thy Name. Thy Kingdom come, Thy will be done, on earth as it is in Heaven. Give us this day our daily bread, and forgive us our trespasses as we forgive those who trespass against us. And lead us not into temptation, but deliver us from evil. For Thine is the kingdom, and the power, and the glory, forever. Amen."

7:00 PM EST, Friday, January 6

The White House

"My fellow Americans, nearly two months ago we witnessed an historic election. The morning after Election Day, House Speaker Paul Ryan assured us that there was no reason to panic; that there was no reason to feel worry or confusion. We could rest assured that although it had been 192 years since this last happened, that our country had been through this before and that the 12th Amendment of the Constitution outlined the process of electing the next president."

"I believe our next president should be Hillary Clinton. I campaigned for her before the election and have continued to encourage members of Congress to support her in the House. I don't think there's ever been a more qualified candidate to be president. Speaker Ryan, of course, has supported Donald Trump, while other members of his party have supported Gary Johnson. This has led to a stalemate in the House. There's also a divide in the Senate which has the responsibility of electing the vice-president."

"Today, after the House and Senate failed to elect a president and vice-president on their first ballots, there was some of that same panic and confusion Speaker Ryan spoke about the morning after Election Day. The market took a sharp decline in the final hour, and many Americans are going into the weekend worried. Banks and ATM machines were running out of cash as people took money out in fear that they would not be able to do so at a later date. Conservative talk radio commentators have speculated that I will try to not leave office."

"But as Speaker Ryan reminded us the day after the election, I am here to remind you today that there is no reason to worry or fret over our future. While the House was unable to elect a president today, remember that Thomas Jefferson, who is today revered by all Americans, was elected on the 36th ballot in the House of Representatives."

"Speaker Ryan was in this office with me just moments before this address. Together, we reaffirmed our commitments to this process. In two weeks, I "will leave this office, and my hope and Speaker Ryan's hope, is that I will leave this office as a new president, elected by the House, is inaugurated."

"A candidate is required to get 26 votes in the House of Representatives to become president. If no candidate has reached 26 votes by noon on January 20th, the vice-president elect, chosen by the Senate, will take the oath of office and will become acting president until that time when the House is able to reach 26 votes for one candidate."

"The Senate reached a vote of 50-50 in the selection of vice-president. Until noon on January 20th, Joe Biden will remain Vice President and in that role he is the tie-breaking vote for the Senate. Earlier today, I spoke with Senate leadership. It is my desire and Vice President Biden's desire that he not be forced to play this tie-breaking role, so for now we will allow the 100 members of the Senate time to reach a resolution on their own without the involvement of my administration."

"Should neither the House nor the Senate elect a president or vice-president by January 20th, I'm still leaving. Let me be clear, because I want to put to rest all of the conspiracy theories on right-wing talk radio. On January 20th, I'm out of here. Should the House and

Senate have not yet elected a president and vice-president, the 12th Amendment of the Constitution then instructs that the Speaker of the House become acting president."

"That means that in two weeks, if the House and Senate have still not elected a president and vice-president, Paul Ryan would then become acting-president."

"I want to assure the American people that from my time together with Speaker Ryan that this is not his desire, and that should he become acting-president, he will continue to work as expeditiously as possible to help the House reach a consensus."

"Having spoken with House and Senate Leadership this afternoon, I can tell you that there is no second vote scheduled in either house of Congress. There is really little point to continued votes that produce no winner. When leadership believes that there has been movement within the membership and that a vote is appropriate, a vote will be called."

"Until then, do not worry. Don't fret, don't panic. While there have been differences between myself and Republican Leadership over the past eight years, and we will continue to have differences, we remain united tonight; united in being fair arbiters of this process."

"If you pray, pray for your country and for your Congress. Be a part of the process. Call or email your representatives in the House and Senate and tell them who you are supporting in this process. But do not fear. You can continue living your life just the way you lived it the day before. Our country has faced many challenges in our history; there are many crises in our national timeline. This is not one of them."

"Thank you, and God bless America."

CHAPTER 16

"He's a pothead. I mean it's a disgrace. I can't believe these representatives are voting for him. I mean what does that say about Congress?" Donald Trump is on a roll the morning after the House vote. He's speaking to reporters at Trump International Hotel in Washington, D.C. He's off the cuff, which means the best of Trump along with the worst of Trump.

Gary Johnson was the highest ranking elected official in the nation, as the Governor of New Mexico, when he came out for the legalization of marijuana in 1999. He was way ahead of his time, but a majority of Americans have now come around to his point of view. Supporting the legalization of marijuana is one thing, but being the CEO of an edible cannabis company, as Johnson was, is quite another. Johnson admits to routinely using marijuana recreationally up until early 2016, but has said he won't use it as president. Johnson hasn't had a drink of alcohol in 29 years because he said he wanted to be a better rock climber and alcohol was holding him back, so his pledge to not get high seems believable. Still, Trump sees this "pothead" as someone out of step with Americans in the heartland, in places like Nebraska and Ohio, whose congressional delegations are now behind Johnson.

This morning at Trump Hotel, he's laying into Johnson, going after him on his positions on terrorism. Johnson is weak, Trump claims, and doesn't understand the threats to our nation. "You want that guy negotiating our trade deals? He'll get out the peace pipe and China will walk all over him. I am tough and I am a good negotiator. We will get great trade deals with me as president. That guy's a pothead."

Trump's strategy publicly has been to not mention Gary Johnson, but after what happened on the House floor yesterday, he's in attack mode. He also has to begin calling out the members of Congress who have jumped ship from Trump to vote for Johnson. They need to feel the wrath, and the rest of Congress needs to see it, lest they be tempted to jump ship as well.

Hillary Clinton is making her move. Trump's once seemingly sure ascendency to the presidency is now in doubt, but if she's going to be the next president, she has to do more than watch Trump supporters switch over to Johnson.

Leading up to January 6th, her staff had several meetings with the relatively unknown, but likeable Republican Congressman from Maine, Bruce Poliquin. Poliquin wasn't enthusiastic about Trump, but it made no sense politically for him to back off supporting Trump now. He'd weathered an entire election cycle and managed to win re-election in a district that voted solidly against Donald Trump. Why go through that and never disavow yourself from Trump, only to do so after you've already secured your re-election and Trump is days away from securing his election?

The only other time in American history that the 12th Amendment was enacted, the election of 1824; the race for the presidency was a four-man race between Andrew Jackson, John Quincy Adams, William Crawford, and Henry Clay.

Henry Clay finished fourth, so with only the top three finishers eligible in the House, Clay was out of the race. Jackson was in the lead in both popular vote and in the Electoral College and it was widely believed that the House would elect him president. Henry Clay, however, was the Speaker of the House and threw his support behind John Quincy Adams allowing Adams to be elected president. Henry Clay became Secretary of State. It's a footnote in American history called "The Corrupt Bargain" and Hillary Clinton is getting ready to make a few bargains of her own.

Poliquin is actually not corrupt. He's a good hearted public servant. Whatever they offer him, he'll have to see it as an opportunity to increase his ability to serve.

Meanwhile, the longest serving Republican in the House, Don Young of Alaska is meeting with Fred Upton of Michigan. Don Young is part of the original Johnson Nine. Fred Upton is a Republican , and the longest serving member of the Republican delegation from Michigan. More importantly, Upton, like Young, is no fan of Donald Trump.

The Johnson campaign thinks they can make a play at Michigan. Republicans have a strong majority there, so it's easier to get a Republican to defect without fear of the state swinging to Hillary Clinton. It's what happened in Ohio all over again. Fred Upton, they believe, is the lynchpin. If they can get him, the others will listen.

Since his appearance with Mitt Romney and the subsequent coming out of the Johnson Nine, Gary Johnson's maneuvers for the presidency have been covert. They've been working on individual members of Congress and targeting specific states. His town halls were a way for more of the public to get to know him, but his case for the presidency was understated.

Now, Johnson and his team are unabashedly making their case. The country is divided. Hillary and Trump are dividers. He can be a unifier. He's a compromise. Even if you don't agree with him on everything, he's better suited to lead a divided country than either Clinton or Trump. With a Republican president, Democrats in Congress will always neatly organize to oppose that president's agenda.

With a Democratic president, Republicans in Congress will do the same. "If you like gridlock, if you are happy with how Washington works, you should support Trump or Clinton," Johnson says in a CNN interview. "But the two big parties won't be able to do that with me. Because I'm not a Republican or Democrat, Congress can actually consider my agenda instead of just looking at whether there's an R or a D in front of my name."

Mitt Romney is back in Washington to meet with Reid Ribble, a Republican congressman from Wisconsin. The Johnson team realizes Wisconsin may offer the same potential as they are now pursuing with Michigan that had been successful in Ohio earlier. Ribble is an influential member of the Wisconsin Republican delegation and Republicans hold a strong advantage in the state delegation. Plus, Wisconsin is the home state of the Speaker of the House. If they can get Wisconsin, it will be a major blow to Trump.

All three campaigns are giving a great deal of attention to four relatively unknown members of Congress from Nevada, where the state delegation is split evenly between two Democrats and two Republicans. Jacky Rosen is a newly elected Democratic representative having just turned over a seat previously held by Republicans. As a freshman congresswoman, she seems hesitant to be brazen and go rouge. She's deeply committed to Hillary Clinton and the money the Democratic establishment offers. The three remaining representatives, Democrat Dina Titus and Republicans Mark Amodei and Cresent Hardy, are all long-time party loyalists. Johnson wants to go after all three. He wants a Democrat to break ranks to show that his support is coming from both sides of the aisle. Hillary's strategy has been to fan the Johnson flames to help him take support from Trump. She could use Johnson to make Trump weak, and then swoop in for the kill. The danger with this strategy is that the flames get out of control. Unaware of Johnson's moves in Michigan and Wisconsin, Hillary is fanning the Johnson flames in Nevada. Through some backchannel maneuverings, they get a commitment from one of the Republicans to vote for Johnson. With two votes for Hillary and one each for Johnson and Trump, Nevada now goes for Hillary Clinton.

In Michigan, Wisconsin, and Maine there are big developments. Bruce Poliquin and the Hillary Clinton campaign have made a deal and when Poliquin switches his vote to Clinton, Maine will go for Hillary Clinton. Don Young's meeting with Fred Upton went better than could have ever been imagined and Upton has gone to work on the Michigan delegation. Now, Upton sends word that he can deliver Michigan. Reid Ribble in Wisconsin assures the Johnson campaign that they have Wisconsin.

Don't think that Donald Trump is sitting idly by and watching his votes slip away. On the first ballot in the

House he was at 25. Each campaign is operating in a vacuum somewhat unaware of maneuverings by the other candidates. After the first vote in the House, Trump is still just one state away from winning the presidency. While Hillary and Johnson have been working to add to their totals, Trump has been out looking for the one single vote he needs.

Inside the campaigns, Johnson and Clinton debate when they should next push for a vote in the House. Will the progress they have made, when made public, help them build momentum? Or, by pushing for a vote, will they be too quickly showing their hand and playing right into Donald Trump's hand?

CHAPTER 17

The Republican National Committee is leaning hard on the Ohio Nine. RNC Chair Reince Priebus lays into Congressman Steve Chabot from Ohio's 1st Congressional District in an obscenity laced tirade. Trump campaign boss Paul Manafort takes a more subtle approach. It's been more than a month since the original Johnson Nine came out. Maybe one of them is experiencing a bit of buyer's remorse.

Manafort goes through the list. Don Young of Alaska is too old. At 83, he's not angling for a cabinet position. Adrian Smith in Nebraska is a possibility, but Jeff Fortenberry is solidly in the Gary Johnson column and Brad Ashford is solidly in the Hillary column, so even if they could get Smith, that moves Nebraska to a push, not to the Trump column. Johnson's poll numbers in Idaho are now at over fifty percent, so getting Idaho to flip back to Trump would be difficult. With Romney's fundraising capabilities and ties to Utah, that state is also a tough nut to crack.

Manafort decides that Kristi Noem in South Dakota is their best target. She's South Dakota's lone representative meaning they only have to convince one person. She's young and attractive and has a bright future ahead of her. If she's smart, she'll realize that this third party movement has no future and that if she wants to be in the game for the long-haul, she'll get back on board with the Republicans.

She's a tough cookie. When she was 22-years old she moved back home to run her family's ranch after her father was killed in a machinery accident. She was once jokingly dubbed "Washington's most powerful intern," in reference to the fact that Noem was serving in Congress while working to complete her college degree, which she did in 2012. And while she may have a libertarian streak, her family ranch has also benefitted from USDA subsidies. She's also staunchly pro-life and can't be too thrilled about Johnson's wishy-washy position on the subject.

Manafort makes a few calls and puts together a team to win back Noem. They're ready to guarantee all the money she'll ever need for future campaigns and lucrative government contracts for her family ranch. If she wants to serve in Trump's administration, there will be a place for her. If she wants to leave the Administration in a few years to run for Governor or Senate, they will support her.

Polls nationwide now have Johnson in the lead with 38 percent. Hillary is in second with 32 percent and Trump is in third with 30 percent. Manafort desperately wants to get Trump to 26 votes in the House before he drops below 30 percent. Johnson's strong numbers have prompted other elected officials to throw their support behind him. California is solidly voting for Hillary, but the eccentric and anti-establishment Dana Rohrabacher, a Congressman from Orange County, comes out in support of Gary Johnson. Rand Paul is in the Senate and doesn't have a vote for president, but he's now in the Johnson camp, as is Rand Paul protégé Congressman Thomas Massie from Kentucky. Where before Johnson was only picking up Congressional support through coordinated efforts targeting specific state delegations, now members of Congress are coming out on their own in support of Johnson. He has momentum, and the Johnson people in the House are pushing for a vote.

Monday, January 9

Following a frantic weekend of maneuvering by the candidates, Paul Ryan announces that the next vote in the House will take place on January 11. The Trump campaign has made some progress with the Ohio delegation. Two of the Ohio Nine Johnson voters have said they'll come back to Trump if they can convince two more. It's not much, but it's something.

A poll is out this morning that puts Trump at 28 percent. Congressman David Bratt of Virginia announces his intention to vote for Gary Johnson. With a delegation split five Republicans to four Democrats, Bratt's support of Johnson means that Virginia is no longer in the Trump column. It's a push, and Democratic vice presidential candidate Tim Kaine, who is from Virginia, is working hard to pick off a Republican from the Virginia delegation.

Wednesday, January 11

Tim Kaine found the vote they needed in Virginia. If you have enough dirt on someone, it's amazing what you can get done. The Trump campaign is in crisis mode. The Ohio Nine will once again support Gary Johnson and the news from Kristi Noem could not be worse. She didn't just say "no;" she's holding a press conference right now where she's laying out, in vivid detail, the goodie bag offered to her by Trump's representatives. "Donald Trump likes to say the system is rigged and that he's an outsider who doesn't play by the rules," Noem says as she wraps up her presser, "His rules include bribery, and I'm not playing by Donald's rules. Donald Trump, this woman can't be bought."

The vote in the House is scheduled for 1:00 PM and there's a sense that something is going to happen. Today could be the day the House elects the next president.

The state delegations caucus and cast their votes.

Republican Bruce Poliquin casts his vote for Hillary Clinton and Maine goes from the Trump column to the Hillary column. In Nevada, a Republican votes for Gary Johnson, so Johnson and Trump get one vote each to two votes for Hillary. Hillary takes Nevada. That's a net gain of two for Hillary, but a net loss of zero for Trump or Johnson as those states were both a push before. However, Hillary takes Virginia by a vote of five for Hillary, three for Trump, and one for Johnson. That's net gain of one for Hillary and a net loss of one for Trump.

Gary Johnson picks up Michigan and Wisconsin thanks to the work of Michigan Congressman Fred Upton and Wisconsin Congressman Reid Ribble. Both were previously in the Trump column.

Speaker Ryan announces the results of the vote:

22 states for Trump, 20 states for Clinton, and 8 states for Johnson. Paul Ryan adjourns the session without any comment on when the next vote will take place.

CHAPTER 18

Meet the Press, Sunday, January 15, 2017

With just five days until we're supposed to inaugurate a new president, there's still no president or vice-president elect. NBC's Chuck Todd has perhaps the most amazing lineup in the seventy year history of the show. First up, Speaker Paul Ryan, followed by all three presidential contenders. Then, Representatives Kristi Noem, Nancy Pelosi, and Peter King discuss the case for each of the candidates and their potential paths to the presidency.

CHUCK TODD: This Sunday on *Meet the Press*. With five days before the deadline to elect the next president, we have the man overseeing that process in the House of Representatives, Speaker Paul Ryan. We'll also hear from the three candidates who are all looking for the votes they need to get the job.

A collection of sound bites play from Johnson, Trump, and Clinton to start the show.

GARY JOHNSON: "The two-party system is dead and you killed it. Americans want to vote for someone and not against someone else."

DONALD TRUMP: "I am with you, I will fight for you, and I will win for you."

HILLARY CLINTON: "I will be a president for Democrats, Republicans and independents. For the struggling, the striving and the successful. For those who vote for me and those who don't. For all Americans."

DONALD TRUMP: "He's a pothead."

HILLARY CLINTON: "A man you can bait with a tweet is not a man we can trust with nuclear weapons."

GARY JOHNSON: "If after four years you decide you're not happy with peace, prosperity, and freedom, you can always decide to vote in another Trump or Hillary."

The montage of sound bites has played and now *Meet the Press* host Chuck Todd is with Speaker Paul Ryan. There are pleasantries and a few softball questions to get things going and then Chuck Todd gets serious.

CHUCK TODD: "Unless something happens very quickly, you're five days away from being President of the United States."

PAUL RYAN: "Acting President."

CHUCK TODD: "The distinction is important to you?"

PAUL RYAN: "Of course it is. The distinction is important to everyone."

CHUCK TODD: "There's not a part of you that wants to be president."

PAUL RYAN: "Nobody in Washington, in an honest moment, won't tell you that he or she hasn't thought about being president; hasn't wished that they were president. But this isn't the way anybody wants to become president. Look, this isn't House of Cards. I'm not Frank Underwood conspiring to get a president to resign. I am trying to get a president elected. Let's say I did want to become acting-president. Let's say that's really my goal. How long do I get to fill that role? What kind of mandate will I have? My goal is to get a president elected as quickly and judiciously as possible."

CHUCK TODD: "Then why is there not a new vote scheduled for the House?"

PAUL RYAN: "I am the leader of a house. In your house, you know the mood of the members. You know when opinions are changing and there's movement in one direction or another. I know those same things in my house, the House of Representatives. If we held a vote today or tomorrow, I can tell you with certainty that the vote would be almost identical to what it was this past Wednesday."

CHUCK TODD: "So you won't hold a vote again until you feel like one candidate has enough votes to win?"

PAUL RYAN: "That's not what I said. If there's significant movement in any direction, we'll likely schedule a vote, so that members and states can go on record with who they are supporting."

CHUCK TODD: "As a Republican, you've supported Donald Trump. Couldn't you manipulate the process by scheduling votes at times that are advantageous to your candidate of choice?"

PAUL RYAN: "I don't think any honest observer of this process could accuse me of that."

CHUCK TODD: "Donald Trump has actually lost support each time the House has voted."

PAUL RYAN: "He has."

CHUCK TODD: "Are you working against Donald Trump?"

PAUL RYAN: "Absolutely not. I am not working for or against any candidate. My job is to be a fair arbitrator of the process."

CHUCK TODD: "You've voted for Donald Trump both times the House has voted."

PAUL RYAN: "Yes I have."

CHUCK TODD: "But on Wednesday when the House voted, your home state of Wisconsin did not vote for Donald Trump. Your home state of Wisconsin voted for Gary Johnson."

PAUL RYAN: "And I will respect the majority decision of the congressional delegation from the state of Wisconsin."

CHUCK TODD: "That sounds like a very guarded answer."

PAUL RYAN: "It's not. I respect the decision of the majority of the congressional delegation from Wisconsin just as I respect the decision of the majority of the congressional delegation from Michigan or Indiana or California or any other state."

CHUCK TODD: "There have been rumors of campaigns offering posts in their potential administrations to members of Congress in exchange for their support. Congresswoman Kristi Noem from South Dakota has accused Donald Trump of offering her a king's ransom. Bruce Poliquin, a Republican from Maine, voted for Hillary Clinton on Wednesday, and his vote was enough to throw Maine behind Mrs. Clinton. What do you make of these allegations? Is this form of bribery taking place?"

PAUL RYAN: If it is taking place, I think it's a very bad idea. The American people are very good at sniffing out corrupt bargains."

CHUCK TODD: "You're referring to the Election of 1824."

PAUL RYAN: "Yes, in 1824, Andrew Jackson won the popular and the electoral vote, but not enough electoral votes to win the presidency outright. So that election, like this one, went to the House of Representatives. That was actually a four-man race. Andrew Jackson was in first, John Quincy Adams was in second, William Crawford was in third, and Henry Clay was in fourth. With his fourth place finish, Henry Clay was out of the running, but he was Speaker of the House. Clay threw his support behind John Quincy Adams, and John Quincy Adams became president. After John Quincy Adams was inaugurated, he named Henry Clay his Secretary of State. The press dubbed it the Corrupt Bargain."

CHUCK TODD: "Do you believe it was a corrupt bargain?"

PAUL RYAN: "I don't know. If you look at the positions of Jackson, Adams and Crawford, Henry Clay was actually most closely aligned with Adams. Maybe he was just supporting the person he thought was best, but that's not how it appeared, or was interpreted. That's why I would say that in this case, the campaigns should avoid even the appearance of impropriety. That's why, other than casting my vote as a member of the Wisconsin delegation, I've remained neutral in the process and have refused to use my position as Speaker to lobby for any candidate."

CHUCK TODD: "Will we have a president by January 20th?"

PAUL RYAN: "I sure hope so. That's what we're working toward."

The candidates appear one by one with Chuck Todd and give their best of talking points. On *Meet the Press*, they're not speaking to any one member of Congress. Their best bet, on this stage, is to win public opinion. If Hillary can build a strong lead in the polls in Pennsylvania, perhaps the Pennsylvania delegation will feel pressured to support her. Johnson now has a strong lead in Colorado, but the Centennial State is still voting for Hillary. Trump wants to win back Ohio, Michigan and Wisconsin, but on *Meet the Press* he's dodging questions about whether or not his campaign offered a deal to Kristi Noem in exchange for her support.

Hillary is questioned about Bruce Poliquin's support. "He represents a district that overwhelmingly voted for me. I think Bruce Poliquin is listening to the voters in his district," Hillary responds.

Congresswoman Kristi Noem has become Gary Johnson's biggest proponent, and Donald Trump's worst nightmare. "Donald Trump believes the presidency can be bought just like he believes women can be bought. If he can write a check to solve a problem, it's not a problem, it's an expense," Noem says calmly. "Donald Trump can't buy me."

Nancy Pelosi takes aim at Gary Johnson. The Hillary Clinton campaign has used Johnson to take momentum from Donald Trump, but now they need that momentum for themselves. Johnson was the gateway drug the Hillary campaign offered to moderate and center-right members of Congress. Now, they need those moderate and center-right members to switch to Hillary.

"His history with marijuana is troubling, and I don't think he takes the threat that terrorism is to our nation very seriously," Pelosi says. "I think he's naive."

Trump surrogate Peter King, a congressman from New York, also hammers Gary Johnson on national security. The message from Pelosi and King on *Meet the Press* is clear. With Johnson's poll numbers now at over 40 percent, it's time for the gloves to come off and for them to take out the insurgent. Pelosi says that Johnson is a political prop of the right-wing Koch Brothers. Peter King says he's out of step with the majority of the American people on social issues. Pelosi says he's too conservatives; he's a radical. Peter King says Johnson is too liberal; an anarchist practically.

"You're all making your case," Chuck Todd says. "You're making your case for your candidate or against another candidate, but how does someone get to 26 votes, because at this point, that looks like a difficult task for any candidate."

"We need the American people to send a message," King responds. The future of our country is at stake. Who are you going to trust our future with? A pot smoking hippie? A corrupt career politician? We need the American people to call their representatives and tell them, for the sake of our future, for the safety of America, to vote for Donald Trump. Let's get this done. Politicians need to stop talking and we need to get this done."

"Well, there's a lot in that statement I agree with, Peter," Pelosi responds, but you're totally wrong on your candidate. Trump is erratic and irrational. We have seen from Hillary Clinton, especially since election night, her calm and confident leadership. These are trying times and Hillary has the experience to lead us. She's not easily rattled. She's at her best in times of uncertainty. I think she's made that clear the past several weeks."

"I've been a Republican all my life," Kristi Noem says in closing, "but I don't know how much longer that will be the case for me, or many other Americans who have identified themselves as either a Republican or a Democrat. The vitriol and innuendo directed toward Gary Johnson today on this show; I am confident the American people will see it for what it is - the last gasp of a dying two-party system."

The next morning an NBC poll has Johnson up two points. He's now at 42 percent nationally.

CHAPTER 19

Politicians are survivors, or they stop being politicians. Now, representatives in several states across the West are torn between two masters: voters and money.

Johnson is now sweeping the Mountain West and is polling at over 50% in South Dakota, Nebraska, Colorado, New Mexico, Arizona, Utah, Nevada, Idaho, Wyoming, and Montana. Of those 10 Mountain West states only four -- South Dakota, Nebraska, Utah, and Idaho -- voted for Johnson on the last ballot in the House. Even Johnson's home state of New Mexico, which he won on Election Night, is a hold out.

Johnson's also over 50% in New Hampshire, where their State Motto is the libertine "Live Free or Die." Johnson is over 45% in North Carolina, Missouri and Kansas and just shy of 45% in Washington State and Oregon. Polling at 45% or 50% among three candidates represents a strong lead, but as of the second ballot in the House, Johnson had zero votes from this collection of six states.

The Senate is still deadlocked at 50-50 in selecting between Mike Pence and Tim Kaine for Vice President. It's now January 18th and there are only two days left to elect a president and vice president. The White House continues to maintain its desire that the 100 United States Senators be the ones to decide who will be the next vice-president. Constitutionally, current Vice President Joe Biden has the tie-breaking vote in the Senate. He could take the drive down Pennsylvania to the Capitol Building and be the tie-breaking vote, but he doesn't want to. Paul Ryan is being prepared to take the oath of office to become the acting president of the United States.

Gary Johnson continues to pick up support in the House, but Speaker Ryan knows his House and he knows it's not yet enough to swing any state one direction or another. Johnson's supporters in the House tout him as the "reasonable choice" or the "compromise." Gary Johnson is the one candidate who could effectively work with whichever vice-presidential candidate the Senate chooses.

Hoping that a vote will force some movement, Paul Ryan announces a vote will be held at 10 AM on January 19 and that if a president is not elected on January 19, which will be the third ballot in the House, a fourth ballot will take place at 10 AM on January 20, just two hours before the deadline to elect a president. If neither the third or fourth ballots produce a president, and if the

Senate has still not elected a vice-president, Paul Ryan will become acting president at noon on January 20.

Johnson has all of the momentum, but still the fewest votes. In politics, money talks.

On January 19th at 10 AM the House Congressional delegations caucus and vote state by state.

Reports of the formation of a new "Mountain West Congressional Caucus" dominate cable news the morning of January 19th and pundits are predicting a major shift in the House vote. New Mexico is now split, one vote for Hillary Clinton, one vote for Donald Trump, and one vote for Gary Johnson. In the rest of the Mountain West, the representatives have gotten the message. Colorado, Arizona, Nevada, Wyoming, and Montana join South Dakota, Nebraska, Utah, and Idaho in voting for Gary Johnson.

The other big shocker of the third ballot on January 19th, though, is Pennsylvania. Joe Biden must have worked some magic in his home state resulting in a shift to Hillary Clinton in Pennsylvania.

The final tally of the 3rd ballot is 18 for Donald Trump, 18 for Hillary Clinton, and 13 for Gary Johnson with one state, New Mexico, abstaining.

The next vote will take place beginning at 10 AM tomorrow, January 20, two hours before the deadline to elect a new president.

CHAPTER 20

It's late; almost midnight on January 19, and Donald Trump is making one more phone call. Since the House adjourned earlier today he's been looking for votes. On Election Night he finished with 269 electoral votes, one short of the number necessary to become president. On January 6, on the first ballot in the House, he finished with 25 votes, one short of the number necessary to become president. He's been losing ever since, and Donald Trump does not like losing. His rallies are like a powder keg ready to explode.

Ohio seems like a lost cause now, but there's hope he could turn Michigan back around. His team still doesn't know what happened in Pennsylvania and members of the Pennsylvania delegation are dodging his calls. The new Mountain West Congressional Caucus is unified. There was a time, a month ago, when Johnson supporters were vulnerable, exposed. Now they find strength in numbers.

There's a call for unity. Earlier this evening President Obama gave his Farewell Address from the Oval Office.

It had many of the usual parts of a presidential farewell address; the parting president touting his record. His speech was also marked with Obama urging one final vote in Congress under his watch. "Elect a president," he urged. He made no secret of who he believed Congress should elect. "During these trying times, nobody is better suited or better prepared to be the next president than Hillary Clinton," Obama said in closing. "That was true on November 8th, and that's even more true now. While the other candidates have been erratic and shaken by this process, Hillary Clinton has been a rock. This is the type of leader we need, and this process has shown us the best of Hillary Clinton. She has been tested and she has been proven worthy."

They're words that make Hillary's supporters happy, but they won't sway one vote in Congress. He's a lame duck.

January 20, 2017

There's pressure to get this done and deals are being made on the House floor. Paul Ryan wants this done. His ability to lead Congress through this process is a reflection of his leadership. He no longer seems to care who wins; he just wants a winner.

The state delegations caucus and the votes are cast.

Trump has lost Missouri, Kentucky, and Florida. Missouri and Kentucky go to Johnson. Florida goes to Clinton. It's now Hillary 19, Johnson 15, Trump 15. It's Hillary's first lead in the House, but there's still no president.

Secret Service and Capitol Police prepare to move Speaker Ryan to the White House to take the presidential oath of office, but he won't go. If he is to become acting president, he will take the oath in the Rotunda of the United States Capitol.

11:00 AM, January 20, 2017

The Senate has also voted this morning and was once again deadlocked at 50-50. There's still no vice-president elect. For one more hour, though, Joe Biden is still the Vice President of the United States. For one more hour, Joe Biden is the President of the Senate, the tie-breaking vote at moments of impasse. At 11:00 AM, Joe Biden's motorcade leaves the White House to make the trip down Pennsylvania Avenue to the Capitol Building.

With a Secret Service escort it only takes about ten minutes to get from the White House to the Capitol

Building. At 11:20 AM Joe Biden is presiding over the Senate and has called for a new vote. One by one each of the 100 United States Senators cast their votes. Senator Tim Kaine votes for himself. With 100 votes cast the total is again 50-50 and Joe Biden casts his vote for Tim Kaine.

And Tim Kaine has just been elected Vice President of the United States.

Kaine announces his resignation from the United States Senate. In accordance with the 17th Amendment, his vacancy will be filled by the Governor of his home state, which is Terry McAuliffe.

Kaine departs the Capitol with Joe Biden and together they return to the White House where his wife and children already await him. They head to the Rose Garden where there will be a small ceremony. Along with Kaine, and his family, the Obamas and Bidens are there. Hillary Clinton and Bill Clinton are there. Hillary wants to be present to see her vice-president sworn in. He'll mind the ship until it's her turn. It's almost noon. John Roberts, the Chief Justice of the United States greets Kaine and asks him if he's ready.

At 12:01 PM on January 20, 2017, Chief Justice John Roberts administers the presidential oath of office with Tim Kaine.

Tim Kaine is acting President of the United States.

Republicans are furious. Congress adjourns for the weekend. It's Friday afternoon, Tim Kaine has been elected vice-president by the Senate and because the House has failed to elect a president, Kaine is acting president.

Republicans accuse Obama and Biden of being manipulative and disingenuous. For weeks they have maintained that they did not want to decide who would be vice-president and then in the final hour Biden swoops in and casts the deciding vote.

But it's done.

Gary Johnson says that Trump can't work with Tim Kaine, but that he can. Republicans in the House feel a new sense of urgency to elect a president. Party loyalty is important, and the party is becoming more unified by knocking Tim Kaine down a notch than they are by the idea of a Trump presidency.

The Mountain West Congressional Caucus is becoming the dominant force in Congress and over the weekend they become the power brokers. Too many states are now in the Never Trump column for Trump to ever be elected president. Too many states are now in the Never Hillary column for Hillary to ever be elected president. Reid Ribble of Wisconsin, who's become a strong Johnson surrogate, meets with one member of Congress after another. "We can keep having votes that end at something like 15-15-15 and we can do that for the next four years. Or we can decide to move on, and there's only one compromise candidate."

Paul Ryan is back on *Meet the Press* on Sunday and announces that there will be another vote in the House on Monday, January 23.

CHAPTER 21

10:00 AM, Monday, January 23, 2017

It's been three days since the House missed their deadline to elect a president, but they're ready to vote again.

Republican Senator Lindsey Graham of South Carolina, a strong critic of Trump, has successfully brokered a deal with the South Carolina delegation and South Carolina moves from the Trump column to the Johnson column. Tennessee and Indiana also go from Trump to Johnson. Pennsylvania, Florida, New Jersey, New Hampshire, Virginia, Oregon, and Washington all flip from Hillary to Johnson.

The fifth ballot in the House is complete. Johnson 25, Trump 12, Hillary 12. New Mexico is a split decision and does not cast a vote.

A representative from New Mexico calls for an immediate revote.

On the 6th ballot in the House of Representatives, New Mexico's two Democratic representatives throw their support behind Gary Johnson. New Mexico becomes Gary Johnson's 26th vote, the decisive vote, the final vote he needed to be elected the 45th President of the United States.

Johnson is summoned to the Capitol. A Joint Session of Congress is convened, the gallery is packed. At 4:00 PM, Chief Justice John Roberts and Gary Johnson take the House floor and for the second time in three days, Roberts administers the oath of office.

"I, Gary Johnson, do solemnly swear that I will faithfully execute the Office of President of the United States, and will to the best of my ability, preserve, protect and defend the Constitution of the United States."

ACKNOWLEDGEMENTS

The idea for this book was over after a few beers at M. Special Brewing Company with my friend Loren Chuchman. I want to thank M. Special for the tasty brews and Loren for his friendship and encouragement with this book.

When you have young children, a book does not happen without the support of your partner. Thank you to my wife Monica for giving me the extra space in our life to write this book. And thanks to my kids for cheering me on even though it meant extended times with my office door closed.

Thanks to my friends (you know who you are) whose excitement for this book helped me to keep writing.

I want to share a heartfelt thanks to my father, Lonnie Vandeventer, for his help with this book. This book could not be possible without him. My dad was the editor but before he edited the book he helped me sort through questions about how the 12th Amendment would play out today. Going back even further, it was my dad who long ago first cultivated in me a passion for politics. This book also became a bridge for my dad and I to reconnect and that alone makes all the efforts worth it. Thanks, Dad.

ABOUT THE AUTHOR

By the time he was 26 years old, Clark Vandeventer was the deputy director of the Reagan Ranch, the historic home of President Ronald Reagan. By the time he was 30, he was a candidate for United States Congress. Clark bet everything on winning but a few months after his failed bid for Congress, he and his young family moved into his in-laws' garage. That's when Clark began the process of rebuilding his life by design.

Today, Clark and his wife Monica, enjoy a lifestyle of design through patchwork income. When they are not traveling around the world, they split their time between Santa Barbara and Lake Tahoe. You can learn more about lifestyle design and patchwork income by reading Clark's book, *unWorking* or visit his blog at FamilyTrek.org.

When he's not writing, skiing, or traveling with his family, Clark is a consultant to nonprofit organizations, training professional staff how to raise big bucks for their causes. You can learn more at MajorGiftsFundraiser.com. Follow him on twitter @clarkvand.

If you loved this book please leave a review on Amazon or wherever else you post book reviews. You can tweet to the author @clarkvand or post about the book on social media with the tag #BackdoorToTheWhiteHouse.

Clark Vandeventer is also the author of *unWorking,* available on Amazon. You can read the preface, introduction, and detailed chapter descriptions of *unWorking* at unWorkingBook.com.

Go to BackdoorToTheWhiteHouse.com to receive emails from Clark Vandeventer for updates on *Backdoor to the White House* and future projects.

www.ingramcontent.com/pod-product-compliance
Lightning Source LLC
Chambersburg PA
CBHW070557180626
46817CB00005B/1887